"So, you are resigned to the marriage now?"

"On certain conditions, yes," Philippa replied, a touch of defiance creeping into her voice. "I keep my home and my salary, and that is all I want when we split up."

"I see." Raoul regarded her thoughtfully. "Well, that disposes of two marriage vows. No perpetuity, no worldly goods. Do you want to discard the clause about forsaking all others, too?"

Philippa shrugged. "Naturally, what you do is your own affair," she said distantly. "I don't expect you to be faithful to me as if I was a real wife."

"You seem to be laboring under a misapprehension," Raoul told her expressionlessly. "You are going to be a very real wife. And *that* is my condition."

Books by Sophie Weston

These books may be available at your local bookseller.

Don't miss any of our special offers. Write to us at the following address for information on our newest releases.

Harlequin Reader Service
P.O. Box 52040, Phoenix, AZ 85072-2040
Canadian address: P.O. Box 2800, Postal Station A,
5170 Yonge St., Willowdale, Ont. M2N 6J3

SOPHIE WESTON

executive lady

Harlequin Books

TORONTO • NEW YORK • LONDON
AMSTERDAM • PARIS • SYDNEY • HAMBURG
STOCKHOLM • ATHENS • TOKYO • MILAN

Harlequin Presents first edition November 1985
ISBN 0-373-10838-9

Original hardcover edition published in 1985
by Mills & Boon Limited

CHAPTER ONE

THE trouble was, thought Philippa Carr, that she already knew too much about him. Raoul de Martin had been making the headlines for years; mostly in the financial pages, admittedly, but his occasional appearance in the social columns had charted a course of light relationships and determined pleasure seeking. A pretty swift mover, her cousin Rupert called him, and Rupert Vivian was no mean socialite himself. It was a major difference between Rupert and herself.

'Wine, Mademoiselle Carr?'

She looked up, startled out of her reverie, into Raoul de Martin's amused golden eyes. She had the disconcerting feeling that he had guessed her thoughts. She shifted uncomfortably, looking away.

'I—would rather not,' she said trying to sound cool and only succeeding, to her own ears, in being prim. 'I suspect I need to keep a clear head.'

Raoul de Martin laughed softly.

'What admirable foresight,' he mocked. The half smile deepened into irony and just a hint of a challenge.

Philippa met the look steadily. 'I do not forget, if you do Monsieur, that the purpose of this meal is business.' She looked round the table at the five other diners, all deep in conversation. 'I suspect that any minute you will start to grill me on this month's sales figures at Vivian Glass,' she added wryly.

He flung back the handsome head and laughed in delight. Then he sobered.

'I already know the sales figures, Mademoiselle. And the state of the order books. And the projections.' The

5

smooth voice had steel in it. 'Did you think that my accountants would be so dazzled by dealing with a gorgeous lady that they would fail to inform themselves thoroughly? I assure you, they know me too well.'

Philippa paled at the veiled insult. It was not the first time that he had said something similar. Presumably he did not like women in business. He must think that a woman's place was on a dance floor or the ski slopes or—occasionally and only if she was fortunate—his bed. Familiar anger rose, as real as bile, in her throat and Philippa strove to control it. She could not afford to offend him. Already Uncle David had asked her, despairingly, to be nice to the man. Vivians was in desperate straits; the merger with Martin Industries was essential if they were to keep going at all. And Philippa, sales director, granddaughter of the founder, mainstay of the office and her uncle's sole support in the last difficult months, prickled every time Raoul de Martin came near her.

She said in a colourless voice now, 'I'm sure they did everything you told them.'

'They did,' he assured her amiably. 'I probably know more about Vivian Glass than you do. I can assure you, mademoiselle, I will not try to trap you into any damaging admissions while under the influence of this excellent vintage.' He poured the pale wine into her glass, ignoring her protest. 'And you must certainly toast the success of the merger.' He raised his glass mockingly. 'To our better understanding.'

This time the challenge was blatantly sensual. The mocking eyes fell to her pale mouth and lingered deliberately. Philippa flinched as if he had leant forward and touched her.

But her voice was calm as she said, 'If that is what you want,' and raised her glass.

The remarkable tawny eyes gleamed for a moment

before he veiled them with heavy lids. He half turned his shoulder on Uncle David and bent towards her as if he wanted to confide something for her ears alone. Philippa dropped her eyes hastily to the wine in her glass that trembled, ever so slightly, in her tense grip. Even so, she knew that the man at her shoulder was laughing.

'What I want is something that you will, I think prefer to leave for discussion for a—er—more suitable occasion,' Raoul drawled.

There was no diplomatic answer to that and she did not dare, for her uncle's sake, to return an undiplomatic one. So she looked away from him, as though she had not heard him, and drew a great sigh of relief when the conversation became general again.

To all outward appearances it was a convivial party in one of the best Paris restaurants. After weeks of negotiation and three intensive days of discussion David Vivian had just agreed in principle to a merger between his small family business and the French conglomerate Martin Industries. David Vivian had faced a good deal of opposition, not least from his son. Rupert Vivian was nominally in charge of public relations. As, however, was widely known in the firm, he did little beyond attending a large number of fashionable functions and presenting the bills to Vivian Glass to settle. And Philippa, who had worked in the business since she left school and was the youngest director on the Board, knew exactly how unable Vivians was going to be to continue to meet Rupert's extensive social bills.

Thinking about it now, she sighed. Rupert was charming but he was an expensive playboy. She did not think, from what she had heard and read in the newspapers, that Comte Raoul de Martin was very different, in spite of his air of wealth and power. So she, too, had opposed the merger that they were now so determinedly looking forward to.

Rupert, of course, was heartily jealous of him. Seeking Philippa out, he had complained to her in great detail about the Martin investigators. Indeed, though he had sulkily refused to accompany his father to Paris for the talks, he had sent Philippa off with instructions to be as obstructive as possible. And Philippa, believing that Vivians could not afford another playboy, had done her best. To no avail. She had telephoned him tonight to tell him so.

'Oh hell, Pipps, is there *nothing* you can do?' he had exclaimed miserably.

'No,' she had said, too tired to try to soften the blow.

He swore fluently. 'You could *try*, for God's sake. Tell him Joe Lamming has sold all our industrial secrets to Caverdons. If all else fails, seduce de Martin.'

It was a despairing attempt at flippancy. Rupert knew better than anyone that Philippa was no seductress. Rupert was quite well aware that Philippa's private life was solitary and celibate and that was the way she preferred it. He even knew why. It had been Rupert, her childhood ally, who had come to her rescue three years ago and had been a constant friend since. He was frivolous and irresponsible but he was fond of her. Moreover, it was his friend, Bob Sebastian, who had hurt and frightened her so badly. Rupert made no secret of the fact that he thought she was turning herself into a frosty spinster, and that he disapproved, but he continued to take her out.

So, instead of taking offence, Philippa said gently, 'He's out of my league, Rupert.'

He gave a crack of laughter. 'Who isn't? The way you go on, you might just as well have joined a nunnery. Oh well, cancel the suggestion. And see if you can fix up a job for me: say barman in some nice friendly nightclub?'

She laughed dutifully and promised to do her best before ringing off. But the plea was more than a joke. It would be difficult for Rupert to keep his so-called job at Vivians after the merger, she knew. And what else was he fitted for? She frowned. She herself had been offered a job by Caverdons, Vivians' major rivals. She had every intention of taking it too, once the sale was complete, as she now had no doubt it would be in time. Perhaps she could persuade them to take Rupert too? She made a mental note to discuss it with both parties.

Her uncle's voice intruded. '. . . if that is all right with you, my dear?'

She jumped, recalled to her surroundings. David Vivian was leaning forward across his host his eyes tired and slightly pleading. She had no idea what he had asked her. She was not, however, going to admit that she had been wool gathering, not in front of Raoul de Martin, who already despised her. So she smiled non-committally and David Vivian sat back, relieved.

It was only later, when the meal ended, that she discovered what she had agreed to do by that smile.

It was after she had gone to fetch her cape. She returned from the cloakroom to the sumptuous foyer to find that only Raoul de Martin and his immediate deputy Frederic Boisson were waiting for her. Of the others, including her uncle, there was no sign. Boisson and his superior were talking in rapid French as she approached.

'. . . not an impressive performance, I agree,' Raoul de Martin was saying in that lazy, amused voice that Philippa was learning to hate.

'But what a surprise. I had heard that the efficiency was tremendous.'

De Martin was wry. 'I, too, was expecting a more dynamic sales director. Still, in a body like that it would be too much to hope for a brain, too.'

Boisson was clearly puzzled. 'But the figures are so

good. And until she took over, sales were falling by the month.'

Raoul de Martin shrugged. 'Let us suppose that the customers stare so hard at her legs they don't notice what they're signing in the way of orders,' he said cynically.

'The legs are truly memorable,' Boisson agreed, grinning. 'And now you get to take them dancing, you lucky devil.'

Philippa stopped dead. She was shaking with outrage. Not because he thought her a fool. To be fair—and she usually managed to be fair even to cynical creatures like the Comte de Martin—she did not blame him for thinking that. She had been stubborn and unhelpful during the negotiations, hoping against hope that Vivians could find another answer to their dire financial problems. And it must be obvious that no other answer could be practicable.

No, she had behaved like a blinkered fool and he was quite justified in treating her as such. What she could not forgive—what crawled over her shrinking self respect—was the light, denigrating way he spoke. As if, she thought, she was not only foolish but utterly beneath contempt.

She took an impetuous step forward. They heard her and turned at once. Boisson's face was a picture of consternation but Raoul de Martin, though he swung swiftly round, did not seem in the least embarrassed. He flung the other an admonitory look and favoured Philippa with a smile of such calculated charm that she could have hit him for that alone.

How dared he abuse her, insult her behind her back and, when caught out, smile at her in that horrid confident manner? Under her cape her hands clenched themselves into very competent fists.

'Ah, Miss Carr,' he said, switching into faultless

English. 'I thought you must have got lost. Your uncle asked me to say good night, as the car was here for him.'

Philippa almost gasped aloud at his effrontery. And then, as she searched for words to tell the charming Comte exactly what she thought of him, the full implication of the change of language struck her. He did not realise that she spoke French. He had conducted the negotiations in English throughout. It had been necessary because David Vivian's French was of the most elementary schoolboy variety. And nobody had asked Philippa what her language abilities were. Raoul de Martin had clearly assumed them to be nil.

For a moment she considered explaining, in the faultless French she had learned from her French grandmother, exactly how much she understood of his uncomplimentary remarks. Then a second thought struck her. If he believed that neither she nor her uncle understood his language he might be tempted to speak unwarily in it. Anyway, here was an advantage not to be thrown away. Perhaps one day she could embarrass him with her facility in French somewhere more public than this.

So, with a great effort, she swallowed her rage and smiled at both of them.

'I am sorry my uncle did not wait for me,' she said, trying not to snap. 'But no doubt the restaurant will be able to call me a cab.'

Boisson exchanged a startled look with his superior.

'But, mademoiselle, you expressed a desire to go dancing . . .'

Raoul de Martin said nothing to support him. His expression was quite unreadable but Philippa had the distinct impression that he knew she had not been listening to Uncle David earlier and had no idea that she had agreed to go dancing when he asked her. She was also positive that he found her plight satisfactorily amusing. So she would not, of course, admit to it. Not that she could face an evening dancing with him, either, not even on a point of honour. The thought of having his hands on her turned her cold.

She said sweetly, 'But I had not realised how long dinner would take. We do not,' with something of a snap, 'take such protracted meals in England.'

There was no doubt, he was laughing silently. She thought she saw his shoulders shake. But he said, gravely enough, 'You desolate me, Mademoiselle.'

She knew he was mocking her. It was only years of practice that enabled her to mask her expression of acute dislike. But she was not a successful sales director for nothing. She gave him her most guileless smile, usually reserved for customers she detested, and looking appealingly at the bewildered Boisson.

'Would you ask them to call me a taxi, Monsieur?'

Raoul de Martin intercepted. 'There is no need for that. I will, of course, take you back to your hotel, Miss Carr. If that is what you wish.'

She shook her head gently. 'I do not need an escort, Monsieur. You need not trouble. I shall be quite safe in a cab.'

'It is no trouble,' he told her solemnly, though his eyes gleamed and she knew that he, as well as she, recognised this as a contest of wills. 'And I promised your uncle that I would take care of you.'

Almost, she ground her teeth. 'I would rather,' she said slowly and clearly, 'that you did not.'

'You have made that very clear,' he agreed, unmoved. 'But I told your uncle . . .'

She said, 'I am myself, Monsieur, not a parcel whose delivery you can arrange with my uncle.' For a moment her control slipped and the venom she was trying to control was plain.

Boisson drew back as if she had spat on him, his

expression dismayed.

'*Mais non, Mademoiselle*, you mistake . . .'

'Gently, Frederic, gently,' interpolated his chief in amusement. 'We are in quite enough hot water with the lady as it is, without you going over the top and telling her she's wrong.' He added in swift French, 'Go home to Simone and the children. I'll see you tomorrow. I'll handle this.'

Boisson looked equally worried and relieved. For a moment only he hesitated. Then, no doubt imagining that Monsieur de Martin could, indeed, handle any woman, he murmured good night and left.

Philippa found that she was shaking with an anger out of all proportion to the incident. Under the cape, she flexed her fingers, trying to calm her temper. No good would be served by precipitating a fight.

'My car is outside,' he told her calmly. 'If you are ready.'

She lifted her chin at him. 'And if I am not?'

The cool golden gaze wandered deliberately from her eyes to her mouth and then down to where she was clutching the cape tight across her breast with fingers that shook. She felt herself flush under that calculated inspection and was furious with herself. He was insufferable. Nobody had ever had this effect on her before. She was trembling as if he had laid those long hands on her.

And then he did just that, reaching out and taking her gloved hand to draw it through the crook of his arm. Instinctively, without thought, she wrenched it away, like a child caught in a playground battle, she thought, bitterly resentful of betraying herself so.

She gave a little artificial laugh. 'I—I'm sorry. I don't care to be touched.' That at least was true, though she did not normally jump as if she had been branded. 'It's something of a phobia of mine.'

His eyes narrowed but he said only, 'Come then, since you prefer to dispense with *all* the courtesies.'

She followed him, shaken at her own behaviour. She could not account for it. Unless it was his looks.

She settled herself beside him in the powerful car, her mouth quirking at the wry thought. He was startlingly handsome and she had not been prepared for it. Was that the reason for her instant hostility? Was that why, every time he looked or spoke to her, she bristled?

For he was, undoubtedly, the most devastating man she had ever seen: taller than Uncle David or Rupert, both of whom were over six foot. Crisp dark gold hair the colour of new minted sovereigns and a tan that made him look as if his skin had been oiled and polished until it glowed. And he moved beautifully, like a runner. In fact he looked like nothing so much as one of the Greek athlete heroes elevated to join the gods for their prowess and fortitude.

Philippa suddenly realised that though she had met him no more than six or seven times and disliked him heartily on each occasion, she could conjure up Raoul de Martin in her mind's eye more clearly than any of her friends or family. Her mouth was suddenly dry and she felt the first stirring of real alarm.

She put a quivering hand to the back of her neck, feeling the tension there. If only he would drop her at the hotel and go. If only she did not have to see him again.

But, of course, he accompanied her into the hotel, summoned up the keys to her room and, before she realised what he was about, had swung her into the upholstered elevator and was steering her to her room.

'What are you doing?' she gasped.

The golden eyes looked down at her enigmatically. 'Taking care of you,' he said with a chuckle. 'As promised.'

He whirled her into the room, followed her, shut the door firmly and set his shoulders against the panels as if he would stay there all night. Philippa looked at him nervously.

'Don't cower,' he told her softly. 'You're brave enough in public.'

She made a helpless gesture. Released, her cape fell from her shoulders, startling her. His eyes flared. She became aware that her pulse was slamming.

She said in a high voice, 'Do you want me to apologise?'

'Apologise?' he mused, almost absently. 'To whom? You would embarrass poor Frederic horribly. And for my own part, though I can imagine wanting a number of things from you, Miss Carr, as I intimated earlier, apologies are not among them.'

Her throat was dry and her voice, when it came, rasped. 'What do you want?'

'An interesting question,' he said lazily. 'I'm not sure I know. Perhaps to test a theory?'

He continued to survey her with that unnerving air of amusment. Philippa tried not to flinch under that appreciative, negligent scrutiny. Her heart was beating so loudly she thought he must be able to hear it. She was bewildered by it. She felt taut as a bow string, mesmerised, threatened and, at the same time, unable to break away. It was like the worst sort of nightmare.

And then he reached for her.

Philippa made a faint protest, a small wordless sound to which Raoul paid no heed at all. Then his hands were on her and she was being impelled towards that towering body as if she were some flimsy thing without strength or will. She had never imagined, much less experienced, such strength.

For a moment he held her, looking down into her white face. Philippa trembled at his expression. Then he bent his head and kissed her as if he had been waiting to do so all evening and could restrain himself no longer.

It was a revelation to Philippa. She had been kissed before, desired before. She had thought herself in love with a man who had found it amusing to lure her into passion. But she had never before felt herself overwhelmed by a tide of feeling that took her far out into depths she had never known existed.

She heard him give a soft laugh, a sound of blatant satisfaction. She was dimly aware that she should resist, free herself and demand his instant departure. But she could not.

His mouth was hard, hungry. There was no forbearance in him, no gentleness, just a fierce demand that she meet and match his sensuality. Her lips parted helplessly.

Her hands were trapped against his chest and she could feel his heart, its steady rhythm undisturbed by the havoc he was wreaking. The heat of his body seared her skin through the silk blouse she was wearing. She tried to turn her head away from that punishing pressure and suddenly she was free—only to find that his mouth was moving with infinite delicacy along her jaw and down the slender column of her throat to where the pulse was racing treacherously.

He paused, as if waiting for some response but Philippa was incapable of speech. Teasingly he brushed his mouth back and forth across the fragile bones of her shoulder. Her eyes closed and her head fell back as the blouse was slipped expertly down her arms. He held her away from him a little so that he could free her wrists from the cuffs.

Her lashes fluttered up and she stared at him, bewildered, hardly aware of the discarded silk. Her ravaged mouth felt swollen. He bent his head swiftly and ran the tip of his tongue along her quivering lower lip.

'Very pretty,' he said mockingly.

His cool fingertips flickered over the exposed whiteness of her breasts with calculated insolence. Her bra was Swiss cotton, modestly cut and embroidered with tiny white flowers. It was a simple, virginal garment of which she was suddenly desperately self-conscious. She bit her lip.

'You certainly don't dress for seduction, I'll give you that,' Raoul went on wryly.

He tossed her blouse casually on to a small gilt chair behind them and turned her back to face him, his hands on her shoulders. Philippa felt that his fingers were branding her flesh. She shuddered, not meeting his eyes.

'On the other hand,' he went on reflectively, 'I don't think I go along with the hysterical virgin story either.'

His hands slipped to her naked shoulder-blades and drew her back against his body. He held her there, doing no more, feeling her tremble.

Philippa was suddenly and shockingly aware of the demands of her own body. It had become suffused with a queer ache, yearning towards this man whom she hardly knew. Her habitual modesty, years of caution, fell away like the blouse he had disposed of. Obeying unsuspected instincts she raised her mouth for his kiss.

Raoul looked down at her, his eyes darkening and she felt a flicker of alarm at what she saw in his face. Then he swooped on her and she reached up to him eagerly returning his kiss without restraint, without thought. Her blood beat. She was dizzy with feeling. His touch was an exquisite delight and she wanted nothing but it should go on and they should be closer, closer.

Her hands were plucking at the buttons of his shirt when he stilled them. Raoul lifted his head and looked down at her, a crooked smile twisting his mouth.

'So you don't like being touched?' he reminded her softly.

She was dazed, the green eyes bemused. He pinched her chin mockingly, as if she was a child or an over enthusiastic puppy.

'That's an interesting phobia you've got there,' he drawled.

For a moment she stared at him, uncomprehending. Then, when the force of his sarcastic remark penetrated her brain, Philippa jumped as if she had been struck and backed away from him, her eyes widening and widening with horror.

Not for years had she allowed a man to get so close. Never had she been so carried away, so unguarded. She felt as if she had exposed herself to the enemy and been mortally wounded in the process. She hunched her arms across herself, retreating.

'What's the matter?' demanded that hateful voice. 'Suddenly realised you were playing the wrong role?'

Philippa shook her head. The soft dark hair brushed against her naked shoulders, reminding her of her state of undress. She gave a small moan of distress. Raoul's face hardened.

'Don't let's have any more play-acting,' he said cripsly. 'Only moments ago you were begging me to take you to bed.'

She flinched.

'Weren't you?'

'I——'

'Weren't you?' Raoul demanded insistently.

She gave a small shrug of hopelessness. It was true. She could not deny it.

'Yes,' she said in a shamed voice.

'And now—as you have a perfect right to do—you've changed your mind.' Raoul's light tone dripped contempt.

Philippa repudiated it with a sharp gesture.

'No. It's not like that.'

'No?'

The golden eyes narrowed, became intent, dangerous. He looked, thought Philippa in alarm, like a predator scenting prey. He smiled.

She shook her head again. 'No. I——'

The smile, which was not a pleasant one, grew. Raoul put a hand to the cravat at his throat and ripped it away in one decisive movement.

'Then let's go to bed,' he said smoothly.

'NO!' Philippa shouted at him.

'But if you want to . . .' he pointed out, unbuttoning his shirt while she watched in horror.

'I don't. I didn't mean that. You know I didn't mean that. You're just being hateful.' The words came tumbling out. 'I'm not like that. I didn't mean . . .'

Raoul stopped undoing his shirt and set his hands on his hips, surveying her grimly.

'Now that I do believe. You thought you'd throw a tantrum. And you didn't expect to have your bluff called.'

He strolled forward.

'You're an interesting specimen, Miss Carr. Nice face. Nice body. And a nasty way of getting your own way. Your uncle obviously hasn't a clue how to handle you. But, as you will have gathered this evening, I am not similarly handicapped. You've had an easy ride up to now, my dear.' He picked up his cravat and looped it round the open collar of his shirt, smiling down at her mockingly. 'This is where it ends. Good night.'

He went out without looking back.

CHAPTER TWO

PHILIPPA drew a breath of pure tiredness as she turned the car into the driveway marked Vivian Glass, the following Friday. The week had been hectic, with her normal heavy schedule increased by the need to talk to the French company's accountants whenever they asked to see her. Which they did, often.

A faint smile dawned at the recollection. Philippa had done her best to answer their questions fully but she had grown increasingly impatient as they returned again and again. And Rupert, breaking all precedents and appearing in his office every day, had been driven to fury by them. In fact she had spent one lunch hour calming him down after a particularly grim session in which the accountants had queried his every expenditure claim for the last six months, according to her indignant cousin.

She hoped he had got over his bad temper or the weekend would be difficult. She had last seen him this morning, still muttering about the high handed attitude of the accountants. She had tried to explain to him that it was normal practice in take-overs but Rupert refused to be calmed down. In his view it was a deliberately calculated insult on the part of Raoul de Martin who, having been forced to give Rupert a job as part of the terms of the contract, was now determined to drive him out in other, more subtle, ways.

At the thought of Raoul de Martin, Philippa's smile died, as it always did. All week, she had been working steadily, forgetting the impending merger and the hateful man who had caused it, and then someone would mention his name and she would go cold with shock. Every time she saw his slashing signature on a piece of paper—and she had seen it often this last week—she felt as if he had reached out and touched her mockingly.

She winced at the thought. Every time she recalled their encounter in her room she burned with self disgust. She tried to put it out of her mind but everything that bore his name reminded her and every time she was reminded that tide of remembered feeling washed over her again, filling her with shame.

She turned the car carefully into the concealed drive entrance to the house, telling herself that at least she would be free this weekend. There would be no Martin Industries' papers, no devoted employees of Raoul de Martin to tell her how Monsieur required things to be done. If she could head off Rupert's complaints and her uncle's admiring reminiscences about the man, she need not think about him again until she went back to work on Monday.

There were a number of cars parked against the ivy covered walls, she noticed with resignation. Aunt Margaret was famous for her dinner parties and always liked to start the weekend with one on a Friday night. Philippa had hoped to arrive after the guests had gone but had clearly failed.

She took her small overnight case out of the boot and went inside. The hall table had been polished to a high sheen and bore a magnificent vase of lilies and ilex. Clearly one of Aunt Margaret's smarter dinner parties, thought Philippa, bestowing her case out of sight under the table.

She cast a quick look in the mirror. She was smart enough, because she had been wearing one of her severe tailored suits to a meeting with clients before she left. But she had that faintly crumpled, weary air. The crisp white blouse was limp, there was a smudge of ink on one cuff and more than a smudge of shadow under the green eyes. Her hair had tousled in the wind, since she had had the roof of her car open on the journey down from London, and now framed her face in a soft tangled cloud. Philippa ran impatient fingers through it, failed to detect any difference and shrugged at her reflection.

She would go and find the party, allow herself to be introduced and then make her escape on indisputable grounds of tiredness. Even Aunt Margaret would not be able to argue with the evidence. She was definitely drooping, she thought wryly.

They were not in the drawing room. So they must still be at dinner. Philippa crossed the highly polished oak floor to the imposing double doors of the dining room and squared her shoulders. She had a natural shyness, unlike her cousin Rupert, and did not like making entrances. She opened the door quietly.

The first thing that she saw was that she had been wrong in thinking dinner was still underway. Clearly Aunt Margaret had decided to leave the gentlemen to their port. The women were presumably upstairs, repairing their make up and gossiping in Aunt Margaret's bedroom. The dining room was full of smoke and Uncle David was pouring port from a Vivian glass decanter.

There were perhaps eight men at the table. They all looked up when the door opened. Philippa, rooted to the spot with embarrassment and something more, became simultaneously aware of three things: the smell of cigar smoke, the glinting of glasses filled with the colour of dark blood, and a pair of steady amused eyes that surveyed her across the table without any hint of the surprise that the others were displaying.

She felt herself caught, mesmerised. It was as if he

had been sitting there all evening, knowing that she would walk in unawares, waiting for her to do it. She froze, her hand on the door handle.

'Philippa, my dear!'

It was Uncle David, unfeignedly pleased to see her, not minding her invasion of his masculine domain. He came round the table to her, both hands outstretched in a gesture of welcome.

'We hoped you would arrive earlier. Your aunt said you might. But in the end we couldn't hold dinner any longer. Was the traffic bad?'

With an effort she dragged her eyes away from Raoul de Martin.

'Not really,' she said, trying for a normal tone.

'Pipps was working late,' interjected another voice. It was Rupert and, she thought, he was already slightly drunk. 'Pipps is a good little executive and doesn't let anything come before business. Not even family,' he said mockingly.

Her uncle looked anxious. But Philippa was used to Rupert's teasing.

'Business is family in our case,' she said equably.

But Uncle David was still concerned. 'Is it true, Philippa? Have you been working all this time?'

'I had a meeting,' she agreed.

'Don't look so worried, Father. You won't have to pay her overtime. She was probably looking for a new job,' Rupert said spitefully. 'Who was the meeting with, sweet coz? Caverdon?'

Philippa stilled. She and Rupert sparred in a good-natured fashion, he complaining of her sobriety, she teasing him about his luxurious lifestyle. And Rupert could be malicious, she knew. But she did not think she had ever heard him use his nasty tongue against her. And it was nothing short of malice to imply to Raoul de Martin that she was selling out to the rival firm.

Her face became masklike. 'A customer, actually,' she said indifferently. 'They want delivery advanced. Very boring stuff by your standards, Rupert,' she added sweetly, for though she was fond of him, she had never let his edged remarks go without a riposte.

Across the table, though she was not looking at him, she knew that Raoul de Martin gave that hateful lazy grin of his. She concentrated on her uncle's pleasant features.

'I'm sorry to have interrupted, Uncle David. I'll go and find Aunt Margaret and tell her I've arrived.'

'We won't be long, my dear,' Uncle David said. 'We'll see you later.'

There was an odd note, almost of pleading in his voice. Philippa's brows drew together. She could not think of any reason why her uncle should wish her to be present, pouring coffee and making small talk, when the men appeared in the drawing room. But his look was almost begging her to be there.

Unless it was part of his campaign to win her over to the impending owner of Vivian Glass? He so admired Raoul de Martin himself, he could not understand that anyone else might not. And of course he was embarrassed by Rupert's unashamed loathing of the man. Presumably he thought that one of the younger generation of the family should make at least an appearance of welcoming the man.

She paused. She had loved Uncle David a long time, ever since he arrived in Paris after her parents had been killed in a car crash. She had been bewildered, frightened: an unnaturally self-possessed eleven-year-old who already knew more about poverty and the scars it imposed on a failing marriage than David Vivian could imagine. And he had been immensely kind. He had gathered her up in a bear hug, bundled her into the car and brought her home to the lovely house, to his kind silly wife who had welcomed her with equal warmth and to the new cousin. She had never been poor or alone since.

She owed him more than a couple of hours being civil to a man she disliked. She would not let him down. Philippa gave her uncle a nearly imperceptible nod. Then, with a vague smile which slid, carefully unfocussed, past Raoul de Martin, she withdrew.

Aunt Margaret was, she discovered, marshalling her forces in front of the coffee tray in the drawing room. She looked up, as Philippa walked in, with a smile of unfeigned pleasure.

'Pipps, my dear, I had given you up. Come to the fire and get warm.'

It was a warm night and the invitation was completely unnecessary. It did not, however, take acute deduction to realise that Aunt Margaret had something to impart that she did not want to announce to the whole room. Philippa went across to her.

'That man is here,' hissed Aunt Margaret conspiratorially, handing her a small cup of coffee.

Philippa accepted it with a little nod. Aunt Margaret, she knew, disliked Raoul de Martin with all the fervour of a doting mother who sees her fledgling dispossessed of the nest by an invader. Aunt Margaret probably made no attempt at all to be civil to him. It was amusing in its way but Philippa found herself sorrier and sorrier for Uncle David. No wonder he had looked so pathetically at her in the dining room. Having insisted on inviting Raoul de Martin for the weekend, Uncle David must now feel he was facing mutiny on all sides.

Aunt Margaret handed her the sugar bowl distractedly. Philippa did not and never had taken sugar in coffee. Aunt Margaret's baby blue eyes were wide with affront and a vague alarm, as if she had suddenly woken up and found herself under threat.

'Oh no, you don't, do you,' she murmured abstractedly as Philippa shook her head at the sugar bowl. 'Oh, Pipps, I don't know what's happening and I'm so afraid. Your uncle was in the most frightful temper before breakfast and he was so *rude* to poor Rupert ...' The blue eyes brimmed suddenly. In Margaret Vivian's perfect world her husband never raised his voice and her son was perfect on every point. 'Then he said that That Dreadful Man had to come down for the weekend and we were all to be nice to him.' She gave a small, ladylike sob. 'I can't bear it.'

Philippa was startled. Her aunt was nothing if not proper: she did not hold with crying in public, much less with making a scene at one of her own dinner parties.

'Do you know what's wrong?' she asked thoughtfully.

Aunt Margaret looked despairing. 'It's business,' she said simply.

She might just as well have said it was a journey to Siberia, Philippa thought in secret amusement. Aunt Margaret had gone straight from her finishing school to being a rich man's adored wife. Business, in her experience, was a foreign country in which the men of her family travelled but where the ladies were not expected to set foot. When Philippa had chosen to go into the family firm, Aunt Margaret had been half appalled, half nervously respectful.

'Uncle David didn't ring me,' she mused now.

Suddenly Aunt Margaret looked uncomfortable, even furtive.

'I think he wants to talk to you tonight, darling,' she said. 'I know it's a bore but you will stay up, won't you? I should think people will go quite soon after coffee. I shan't,' she added naïvely, 'offer them a second cup.'

Philippa laughed, draining her own. 'Not even me?' she teased.

Aunt Margaret considered that seriously. 'Well, of course if you want, darling. But hadn't you better go and change before the gentlemen join us? You won't want to look grubby.'

Philippa stood up obediently. 'You mean you don't want me to look grubby,' she corrected affectionately. 'All right, pet, I'll do what I can.'

In the room which had been hers ever since Uncle David first brought her back from France, she surveyed herself ruefully in the dressing table mirror. There was not a lot, she thought, that she could do. Her face was too thin, with a pointed chin that made her look—when she was in a good mood—like a mischievous elf and, when she was not, like a witch. She was too pale and this was accentuated by the heavy dark brows and long, long eyelashes. And her eyes, no matter what her mood, were a clear unwavering green. They were widely spaced and could be expressive. Their habitual expression, however, was cool and guarded.

They were particularly guarded now, as she climbed into a simply cut cocktail dress, the colour of Uncle David's old port. She brushed her hair till it shone and coaxed it to fall, with apparent casualness, about her face. Then she did what she could with cosmetics to add colour to the pale cheeks, a hint of glitter to the eyelids. But none of it, she thought, sighing, was any use. Raoul de Martin would not look at the serene and shining mask. He would look straight into her eyes, recognise the wariness there and, damn him, be amused by it.

She went downstairs slowly, wondering how she had come to know, with such absolute conviction, what Raoul de Martin's reaction would be. It implied a degree of rapport between them which, instinctively, she rejected. She did not want to understand Raoul de

Martin; and, more than anything in her life before, she was afraid of the thought that he might understand her.

She had learned self control at an early age, though, and nothing of her thoughts showed in her face when she re-entered the drawing room.

Instantly she was greeted with a little scream of welcome by Sybil Langton, wife of a locally resident journalist. Sybil was not a close friend of hers and, as the conversation progressed, Philippa began to entertain the suspicion that she was being expertly pumped for information about the firm and Martin Industries. She became very non-committal, parrying Sybil's questions as coolly as she could, but she was startled.

'And have you known that lovely man long?' gushed Sybil.

'Raoul de Martin?' Philippa raised those dark brows in eloquent surprise. She managed to sound both aloof and faintly amused, a feat of which she was justifiably proud. 'Long enough.'

'Isn't he the sexiest creature you have ever seen?' pursued Sybil, undeterred.

Philippa pretended to consider that. 'One of them,' she allowed.

Sybil tittered. 'Oh you! You're spoilt, with the gorgeous Rupert in the house all the time. Some people have all the luck.'

She broke off, confused. Looking up, Philippa realised with a sharp little pang of embarrassment that Raoul was standing behind them and must have heard their remarks. She felt herself flush faintly.

And then, incredibly, he reached out a long finger and laid it against her hot cheek. Bemused, Philippa heard him say mendaciously that she had promised to show him the garden. Indignantly aware of Sybil's avid eyes and the fact that she could not dispute the point with him without letting Uncle David down, she rose in a daze and followed him.

'Perfection,' he said when they were outside. 'So English.' He gave a soft laugh. 'The plain clothes, the simple hair.' He brushed her cheekbone with the back of his forefinger, very light. 'The perfect skin.'

Philippa jumped. The caressing note was still unmistakeable in his voice. Since she had every reason to know he disliked and despised her, she could not account for it. Unless it was for the benefit of someone other than herself. She looked round the twilight terrace uneasily. There was nobody there but themselves. The windows into the drawing room stood open and a faint murmur of conversation floated out. There was no possibility that they could be overheard.

She said stiffly, 'I don't understand why you are doing this.'

'Mmm?' The errant finger continued to trace the bone structure of her face. 'Doing what?'

Philippa turned her head away impatiently. His hand fell.

'Flirting with me,' she said in disgust, scornful as much of her response as his ability to arouse it.

'Alas, only trying to flirt with you,' Raoul said in amusement. 'You're very English about that too.'

Although he had taken his hand away, the disturbing golden eyes were still on her. Philippa felt confused, breathless. She tried to take hold of herself.

'English?'

Raoul settled happily against the stone wall and crossed his arms over his chest, as if about to embark on an interesting debate.

'It is always said that English women do not understand the art of flirting,' he told her kindly. 'That they are too unsubtle. Too cold, perhaps. Too much in command of their emotions.'

'And you think I am?' Philippa was wry. She had hardly been self-possessed in her dealings with Raoul de Martin.

For a moment he did not answer her. She had the feeling he was weighing his words and that, in the event, decided to withhold what he had debated telling her.

'I think that sometimes you would like to be,' he said carefully.

'I don't follow.'

'No?' He gave a sigh. 'Let me put it this way. I think you admire the coolness of, for example, your aunt. You emulate her. You are both very polite, very remote.' His voice hardened. 'Perfect manners and no heart. I think you would like to be like that, *ma petite*.'

She stared at him, fascinated. She should have been offended. This low voiced, academic discussion of her character should have insulted her beyond bearing. Aunt Margaret would have thought it very undignified, Philippa knew. Raoul's analysis was right to that extent.

She said flippantly, 'Are you telling me my manners are frightful but my heart is in the right place?'

Raoul considered her unsmilingly.

'By no means. I remain to be convinced that you have a heart. But I do know that—sometimes—you are not quite as much in control as you would like,' he told her with bite. 'I find it—interesting.'

So she was an interesting specimen. Well, what else did she expect, Philippa asked herself. This man probably had so many women processing through his life that he could only differentiate them by such observations.

But why was he bothering with her at all? What did he expect to gain?

She said abruptly, 'What's going on, Monsieur de

Martin? I did not expect to see you here this weekend ...'

'Or you would not have come,' he interjected,
nodding as if in agreement with something she had
herself said.

Philippa raised startled green eyes to his face and he
smiled crookedly.

'I am aware of that, *mignonne*. I am not a fool.'

'B-but why then ...'

He shrugged, swinging away from the wall and
descending the shallow steps that led from the terrace to
the path and thence to the sundial in the middle of the
lawn. As if drawn, she followed him. He did not touch
her, though she half expected him to take her hand. It
was oddly disappointing that he did not.

'Business,' he said succinctly. 'Things do not go as
well as they might. I am sure you know why.'

Honestly puzzled, Philippa shook her head.

'No, I've no idea. We've all co-operated with you
accountants. Has something else gone wrong with
production?' she asked, knitting her brows.

He looked faintly scornful. 'Do you really not know?
Do you not read the financial press?'

She hesitated, pausing beside a lavender bush whose
heady scent rose on the evening air. The gentle scents of
the garden were in stark contrast to this sophisticated
man and his talk of business. She surveyed him
candidly.

'Not when I'm hoping for a peaceful weekend,' she
told him, her voice rueful. 'But I can see that you think
I should have done. You'd better tell me what the
papers are saying.'

'They are saying,' he told her with narrow-eyed
precision, 'that Vivian Glass is insolvent and Martin
Industries is buying at a knock down price. Which,' he
showed his teeth in a savage smile, 'is not very good for

the share price of either, as you would have seen had you read the paper this morning.'

Philippa took it calmly. She had learned the value of calm while working with her temperamental uncle.

'It must be pure speculation. The papers don't *know* anything.'

'The papers,' he said silkily, 'seem to be singularly well informed.'

That startled her. Her head came up sharply.

'But who——?'

'I thought you might help me on that one. I rather thought your beautiful cousin Rupert,' Raoul said casually.

'No!' It was a protest rather than denial. Philippa could easily imagine Rupert running to the press with any story, however damaging, when he was in one of his reckless moods. Had she not seen this evening how hostile he was to de Martin?

'No?' he echoed, raising his brows.

'It would be stupid,' Philippa said after a moment. 'It would harm everyone, including himself. Rupert's got a lot of Vivian shares.'

'Ah yes, the English phrase: cutting off his nose to spite his face, is it not? But do you really think that the beautiful Rupert has the intelligence to realise that is what he would be doing? I think you overestimate him.'

Philippa could see there was no point in trying to defend her cousin.

'What are you going to do about it?' she asked. 'A press statement?'

He hesitated, the heavy lids drooping. An enigmatic smile played about the beautifully sculptured mouth. He said carefully. 'That is a possibility, yes.'

'Saying what?'

'Ah,' he looked about him, sniffing the air

appreciatively. 'How beautiful this is. Let us not talk about such things. Tell me instead about this wonderful garden which you love.'

Philippa looked at him doubtfully. There was something more, she knew, something he was deliberately withholding from her. And she also knew that she was helpless to extract from him more than he wanted to tell her.

She gave a small shrug and allowed herself to be led along the paths and walks of the famous garden while she discoursed somewhat absently on roses and jasmine and syringa. To all of which Raoul listened with grave attentiveness. It redoubled her suspicions.

Nor did he attempt to touch her again once they were out of sight of the house. Philippa was surprised and, she found, not at all relieved. She had the feeling she was being used without her knowledge. It worried her— this change between the last time they had met when he had given every indication of despising her and this odd detached courtesy. And he kept watching her. All the time. As if she were an animal that he thought might suddenly bolt.

She was relieved to return to the house, though her suspicions were not quieted by the fact that, on their entrance, Rupert cast her a look of disgust, swallowed his brandy in one gulp and turned on his heel, slamming the door behind him Raoul's face was expressionless but she had the oddest feeling that Rupert's display of temper had given him an obscure satisfaction. He is manipulating us all, she thought, chilled.

She crossed over to her uncle who was holding what appeared to be a rather desperate conversation about fishing with the inquisitive Langtons. She touched his arm.

'I'm tired. I seem to be going muzzy,' she said to

them cheerfully, suppressing her disquiet. 'I think I must go to bed, Uncle David.'

He drew her away from the Langtons, murmuring an excuse, offering her a cigarette. He looked anxious. 'Don't do that my dear. I'd hoped for a word with you.'

'Tomorrow,' she promised. 'And I'll just slip out. I won't break up the party.'

He did not smile. 'Pipps, I really must see you tonight. It's urgent,' he said in an undervoice.

She was alarmed but she smiled steadily.

'It can't be so urgent that it won't wait until morning,' she protested. 'The business isn't going to go bust overnight.'

David Vivian looked even more unhappy.

'It's more than that. It's ... oh, look Pipps, if you can't bear to wait up, and I don't blame you for that—can you come along to my study now?'

'Now? But surely if you leave it really will break up the party.'

He shrugged. 'That's Margaret's problem,' he said with uncharacteristic callousness. 'I wouldn't have had any of them here this weekend but she insisted. I expect, like every other damned disaster, it's the boy's fault,' he added with such concentrated bitterness that Philippa was silenced.

'All right,' she said gently. 'If it's so important.'

They retreated quietly, watched with anxious, but surprisingly unreproachful eyes by Aunt Margaret. Normally she would have protested vigorously against her husband and niece quitting the drawing room before the departure of her guests, particularly as Rupert had already abandoned good manners and stormed out of the drawing room earlier. But Aunt Margaret was quiet as a mouse as they left.

In David Vivian's study, they sat uneasily, on either side of the marble fireplace. For a few moments he puffed nervously on his cigar, tapping the ash into the pile of logs, even where no ash had accumulated on the tip.

At last he said jerkily. 'We're in the devil of a hole, Pipps. Rupert can't have *realised* ... But there's no point in talking about it; it's done now. If we don't do something quickly there'll be nothing left.'

Philippa said nothing. He gave her another of those quick, pleading looks, and then transferred his gaze back to the unlit fire.

'You're the only hope, Pipps. I don't like it. I shouldn't ask you. I told him I wouldn't. But he's right. There isn't any other way.'

She sat very still. 'Other way?'

'Out of this mess with the papers. They've been ringing up all day. If we don't do something we shall have to ask for the share quotation to be suspended, Geoff says, and then God knows what will happen. Complete collapse probably.

Philippa's mouth was dry. She swallowed. Geoff Lane was their accountant.

'And what does Geoff think *I* can do?'

David Vivian gave her a quick, ashamed look.

'Not Geoff. Raoul. Raoul de Martin,' he muttered.

'What,' repeated Philippa gently, 'am I supposed to do to avert disaster?'

Her uncle clasped his hands together so hard that she saw they were shaking with tension. The cigar, unconsidered, dropped its ash on the elegant rug.

'Marry him,' said her uncle at last on a desperate rush.

CHAPTER THREE

'MARRY him!' Philippa sprang to her feet, her face whitening. 'Uncle David, you can't be serious.'

Her uncle did not look at her.

'It's the only way, Pipps. A quick announcement now, tomorrow morning, and everyone would say that of course Raoul's visits over here were to see you and even when the merger was eventually announced they would only think it natural because of the family link.'

He spoke rapidly, tonelessly. Philippa had a tiny suspicion that he was reciting a lesson that had been taught him by someone else. She bit her lip.

'What if I agreed to an announcement? A notice in the forthcoming marriages columns, or whatever. Wouldn't that be enough? We could call it off later. Lots of people do.'

David Vivian shook his head.

'I've suggested that, Pipps. It won't work.'

'Why not?'

'Because you don't go merging companies on the basis of marriages that haven't taken place,' he said almost with exasperation.

'But——' She broke off, slipping bonelessly on to the library steps, clutching at the wooden column with fingers that shook. 'He would never agree,' she said at last in desperation. 'Raoul de Martin. He would never get married, even to support his company. I'm sure of it.'

Uncle David gave a bleak smile. 'It was his suggestion,' he said gently. And, as she stared at him in dismay added, 'I doubt if he'd get married for any other

36

reason. He likes his bachelor life. It gives him everything he wants. He is only contemplating marriage to save Martin Industries. And,' he added with point, 'Vivian Glass.'

Philippa's head sank. She rested her brow against the back of her hand while her fingers clenched tighter and tighter round the polished wood. Her uncle watched her in silence, his expression an unstable mixture of compassion and impatience.

At last she said in a muffled voice, 'Please don't ask me to do this, Uncle David.'

'I have no alternative, my dear.'

She said, 'I don't like him. I don't trust him. And I don't want to marry. You know I don't. Why didn't you tell him that?'

She sounded, even in her own ears, like a peevish child. Her uncle was unimpressed.

'Pipps, we're not talking about ordinary circumstances,' he said wearily. 'I doubt if he likes you all that much, either. But he's prepared to do it—for the good of both companies. All right, I know that you have never wanted to marry. But, don't you see that is an advantage in this situation? There isn't anyone else that you're in love with, is there?'

Philippa did not answer. Her uncle looked at the bowed shoulders doubtfully.

'At least, there's nobody else whom you want to marry. Obviously, if someone comes along Raoul would give you your freedom.'

She raised a white face.

'Obviously?' she asked drily.

David Vivian was shocked. 'But of course. He's a civilised man. A divorce—in time—would be perfectly acceptable. You might both prefer it anyway, after a couple of years. When the company is on its feet again and sales are back up to target.'

Her lips felt cold and stiff as if anaesthetized. She said with an effort, 'And in the meantime?'

'In the meantime you're married. But, good God, Pipps, you're not a child. You can set whatever terms you want, as to where you live, where you work, how much you see of each other. Just talk to him about it . . .'

'No.' It was barely voiced but it had a force which stopped David Vivian in mid flow.

He began to look really anxious.

'Pipps, I've never asked you for anything before.'

She put a hand to her shaking mouth.

'I know,' she said wretchedly.

'If this merger doesn't go ahead, the company will close down. Men who have worked for Vivian Glass all their lives will be out of a job. With no prospect of another one.'

'I know,' she said again.

'Your aunt and I will have to leave this house. If the shares lose their value we will have nothing. It would break Margaret.'

Philippa's head sank lower.

'Pipps, if we were asking you to leave someone you loved—or if we were asking you to make a real marriage—I wouldn't do it,' he said with emotion. 'But it isn't like that. It's a charade. A pretence on both sides.'

Philippa could bear the pleading note no longer. She stood up abruptly.

'I'll think about it.'

He was not satisfied but he realised that it was as much of a concession as he was likely to get out of her.

'And you'll talk it over with Raoul before you make up your mind?'

She gave an instinctive shudder which he could not have missed. He averted his eyes.

'He's not a bad chap, you know, Pipps. I know you

and your aunt don't like him but he's not a villain,' he said awkwardly. 'He's been very honourable about the merger.'

'And you think he would be very honourable about an unwanted marriage?' she flashed.

His sad eyes filled with pain.

'Don't talk like that, Pipps. You sound so hard.'

She stared at him until he began to shift uncomfortably under that direct gaze.

Philippa said softly. 'I *am* hard, Uncle David. I've been made hard. And this scheme of yours is not exactly designed to be undertaken by one of your soft and feminine women, is it? I think you ought to thank your lucky stars that I am hard, not complain about it.'

He made a helpless gesture.

'You're making this very difficult for me. What else am I to do? I have to do what I can to protect my wife, my son, the men who work for me. Can't you see that?'

'Even if it includes human sacrifice?' hissed Philippa, shaken by the hurt and betrayal she felt.

She would have trusted him with her life. At an early age, experience had taught her to be cautious of other people but, thought Philippa wearily, she had never had that carefully wrought guard up against Uncle David. He had welcomed her, seemed to hold her in affection. She had not been at the centre of his world where Aunt Margaret and Rupert were but she would have sworn that he would never do anything to hurt her. Until, as she now realised, Aunt Margaret and Rupert were threatened. The fight went out of her.

'I must go to bed,' she said in a dead voice. 'I'm so tired I can't think straight.'

'Yes, that's probably true.' Her uncle was eager to ascribe her outburst to fatigue. It relieved him of some of the feelings of guilt, she could see. 'You'll see things clearer in the morning.'

She shrugged, giving a faint, mirthless smile. 'I see them pretty clearly now. But by the morning I may know what I'm going to do about them,' she said going to the door.

'Pipps.' The pleading note was back in his voice. He was begging her forgiveness, some sign of compassion from her. But Philippa was still too heartsick. She could not bring herself to cross the rug again and kiss him good night as she usually did.

She avoided his eyes. 'Good night Uncle.'

She went noiselessly out of the room, closing the door with infinite care. Nevertheless, she heard a distinct sound and, looking up, realised that the companion door into the other half of the library had also been closed. In the brightly lit passage Raoul de Martin was standing outside the other door as if he had just emerged. The expression on his face was graver than she had ever seen it.

Philippa jumped and, with her uncle's words still ringing in her ears, blushed.

He said her name very softly and gently as if she were a frightened animal he was trying to lure to come towards him. The implications of his sudden appearance, his reassuring manner, suddenly hit Philippa. She stared at him.

'Were you in the library?' she demanded. 'Just now, when I was talking to my uncle?'

He did not attempt to dissemble. 'Yes.'

'How much did you hear?' Her voice cracked.

Raoul's mouth twisted. 'Rather more than I'd have liked, to be honest.'

'You were eavesdropping,' she accused venomously, in an agony of embarrassment at what he had overheard.

He shrugged. 'Not intentionally. I wanted to talk to your uncle and by the time I realised you were still with him it was not possible either to interrupt or to retreat.'

She felt exposed, humiliated. She was furious with her uncle for putting her in this position and more than furious with this man who stood looking at her with spurious concern. Philippa tilted her chin and looked him straight in the eye.

'Well, it saves time, I suppose. Though I would have preferred not to be spied upon. At least you will be in no doubt as to my feelings on this—proposition—of yours.' She was proud of her tone: not only did her voice not shake but she managed to drip contempt.

She thought Raoul's eyes darkened; for a second he looked as if he might even have been hurt by the remark. But then he was himself again, cool and unreadable.

'Yes,' he agreed in that equable voice. 'Your feelings were made very clear.'

'Then,' she was hesitant, 'you'll forget all about this idea?'

'Marriage you mean?' Raoul shook his head. 'I'm afraid not.'

'But if you know that I hate the thought,' Philippa began heatedly but was interrupted.

'I always knew.' He sounded oddly weary. 'Your feelings come as no surprise to me. I did not propose this rush into matrimony because I thought you'd welcome it but because it is the only solution to a problem which is rapidly approaching crisis proportions. I am sorry, of course, that you are so upset. But I'm not exactly ecstatic about it myself.'

Looking hard at him, Philippa discovered that she thought he was speaking the truth. The magnificent vitality of the man which she had remembered so vividly seemed dimmed. There were deep clefts running from nose to the corner of his mouth almost as if he were in pain and controlling it only by an effort of the will. And his eyes were tired. She was surprised that she had not realised earlier how worn he looked and felt remorseful.

'I'm sorry,' she said, as she had not been able to say to her uncle. 'I can see it's a tough problem. It's hard luck that the papers got hold of it.'

'It was not luck,' Raoul said grimly. 'It was your cousin Rupert.'

Philippa froze.

'And that's the other thing your uncle did not mention. I suppose he was too ashamed. Though he knows it for the truth as well as I do. So you see——' he said softly, '—Vivian Glass owes me a debt.'

She stepped back, her feelings of sympathy ebbing.

'Which you think I ought to pay?' she demanded.

His smile was slow and infinitely threatening.

'Which I intend to see you *will* pay,' he told her quite gently. 'Make no mistake about it.'

Philippa had no answer. She was shaken by the determination she could see very clearly in his face. She remembered that she had once told her aunt that there was nothing to be gained from appealing to this man's better nature. Now she realised with a shiver how right she had been. He was without pity. He was owed and he would collect, no matter at whose expense.

She said in a low, horrified voice, 'You're vile.'

Again that swift, Gallic shrug. 'Maybe. At any rate I'm not destroyed by hard names. You will marry me.'

Her throat was dry. 'And afterwards?' she managed.

The unreadable gaze passed slowly over her in a deliberate, insulting assessment.

'Afterwards,' Raoul said, his accent deepening, 'we will reach an accommodation.'

Philippa was tired and full of grief. She wanted nothing so much as to crawl into her room, barring the door against all comers, and lick her wounds in private. She was not, however, going to leave this arrogant man with another victory to his score.

So she smiled at him with false sweetness and said, 'An accommodation on what terms?'

He bowed politely. 'Mutually acceptable ones, I hope.'

'I see you already have something in mind,' she said calmly.

He gave a faint ghost of a laugh. 'I have indeed.'

'Excellent. Then you can outline the terms to me tomorrow. Before,' she explained as she swung past him and up the sweeping staircase, 'I decide.'

She did not look back to see his response to her demand. She was glad enough to escape from him with the last word and some vestige of dignity still intact. And, to her enormous relief, the tears did not break out until she gained the sanctuary of her own room.

Symbolically she turned the heavy brass key in the door. She did not really believe that anyone would follow her. They had all, she thought in bitter amusement, had their say already. And she was bereft. Once more she was reduced to being a bewildered counter in games that other people played and she did not really understand. All the illusion of affection which the Vivian family had conferred on her was revealed, under the cruel spotlight of Raoul de Martin's plans, for the transparent thing it was; without substance, to be discarded at a stroke when more important interests were threatened.

Philippa went to the window and looked unseeing out into the garden. All was blackness except for the grey sky behind the gigantic shapes of trees. The warmth of the still day hung in the air like incense. Not a bough or leaf moved. Philippa put a hand to the back of her neck, easing the tension she felt there, aware of the

oppressive quality of the atmosphere. Perhaps there
would be a thunderstorm.

She shrugged, turning away from the window. Her
aunt detested thunder, having to be comforted with
warm drinks and company during a storm. Sometimes,
if the lightning came close, she even had to be sedated.
Tonight Philippa would not be one of the anxious
family members soothing Margaret Vivian's fears. She
had never felt so isolated from them before, not since
she arrived here all those years ago.

The green eyes darkened with pain. Her arrival was
something she preferred not to think about, along with
the years that preceded it. Her mother, Uncle David's
sister, had never got used to the life of the wife of a
struggling violinist. She had become peevish, querulous,
constantly complaining of minor ailments. And Leon
Carr had suffered for it.

Philippa's hands clenched as she remembered her
beloved father. He had been brilliant but mercurial. He
had needed a wife who believed in him, who supported
him with steady good humour and built up his
precarious confidence. Instead he had found Julia
Vivian, a spoilt wayward child who cared little for
music and understood nothing of his torments of self
doubt. Julia had married a dashing, handsome young
man and could not wait for him to become an
international celebrity. Every enthusiastic review had
her out in the grand shops of Paris buying clothes Leon
could not afford to pay for. Every lukewarm review
brought tearful reproaches.

All Philippa could remember of the marriage was her
parents' quarrelling. However insensitive she might be
to her husband's feelings, Julia had known him well
enough to aim her barbs so that each one struck home.

They were killed on the motorway from Lyons,
returning late one night after a concert at which her

father had been principal soloist. Philippa had little doubt that they had been arguing when the car skidded and turned over. Ironically, the notice in the next day's newspapers had been full of praise for Leon's performance. He had, said the critics, found himself at last.

She sat down at her dressing table and began, wearily, to cream off the make-up so recently applied. As she had expected, it had done nothing to disguise her feelings from Raoul de Martin.

She put the cotton wool pad down carefully, noting, as she did so, that her hand was shaking, like ripples on the surface of a calm stream. What was there about the man that harried her so? Was she really frightened of him?

Philippa folded her hands together hard, trying for composure. There was nothing he could do to her, she told herself. He could not force her to marry him. She smiled at the thought of his dragging her to the altar but was serious again at once.

The truth was that she did fear something of the sort. Oh, not that he would manhandle her or subject her to violence but something more insidious, less easy to deflect and infinitely more difficult to withstand. She bit her lip. He knew as well as she did that she was powerfully attracted to him. He had demonstrated as much to both of them. He would not, she thought, hesitate to use that knowledge against her.

She shut her eyes. And then she would not be able to call her soul her own. It would be as bad as it had been after Bob left. No, it would be worse because, although she had misjudged Bob and in the end been cruelly betrayed by him, she had really for a while thought herself in love. But this thing with Raoul de Martin had no politely acceptable face; there was no hint of romance about it. Plain lust, that was what it was, and

Raoul de Martin was not likely to mistake it for anything else. Or, she acknowledged drearily, to want anything else. Any more than Bob had done.

They were two of a kind, she reflected, Raoul de Martin and Bob Sebastian: witty, sophisticated, charming—and profoundly cold. Well, she had cried herself dry after Bob's callous behaviour. She was not going to cry over Raoul de Martin. If she married him—and at the moment she could not really see an alternative—it would be on her own terms. And those terms would make very clear what was her exclusive territory and where he was not to trespass.

She went to bed, curling herself up into a tight ball and shivering, although the night was far from cold. She despised herself; she willed herself, with furious intensity, to forget the whole matter and concentrate on sleep. But every time she began to drift off the thought returned to her, in all its sinister implications, that Raoul de Martin had manoeuvred her into accepting him where she had accepted no other man in her life.

When she slept at last there were tears on her face.

CHAPTER FOUR

In the morning she got up early after her disturbed night and slipped out into the woods. She walked for hours, it seemed, getting her ankles soaked in the dew-wet grasses. It was not that she was trying to make up her mind—she had seen what her decision must be all too clearly last night—but she had, somehow, to reconcile herself to the abrupt, unwelcome diversion of the course of her life.

By the time she returned to her house she was resigned, though her face still wore a look of strain and there were shadows under the lovely eyes. They did not escape the attention of Shelley, long time housekeeper in the Vivian abode.

'You look as if you need a good breakfast,' she told Philippa astringently. Privately she thought that what Miss Philippa needed was a good man to take some of the responsibility for that damned firm off her shoulders. Mr David was past his prime and young Rupert had never been more than a fly-by-night. That tall Frenchman, now, he was the sort of man to do it. 'You go and sit on the patio in the sun and I'll bring your breakfast out,' Shelley concluded craftily.

Philippa thanked her and did as she was bid, all unsuspecting. And then, as she went round the corner of the house, she stopped dead in her tracks.

Raoul de Martin looked up, smiled and courteously rose to his feet at her approach. As always, she had a little shock at how tall he was. This morning he was wearing light-weight denim pants and a pale shirt which, as a concession to the increasing heat of the sun, was rolled back from his wrists and open half way down the front. He looked tough, competent, and, as Sybil had said last night, frighteningly sexy. Philippa swallowed hard before she got up her courage to approach him.

'Good morning,' he said with a smile. 'You're up early.'

'I had things to think about,' Philippa told him gruffly.

Raoul looked ever so slightly amused. 'I remember,' he murmured.

Philippa knew she was being laughed at and decided to take the wind out of his sails. 'And I've thought. So you'd better go ahead and announce the engagement. It's not what I'd have chosen but I don't see an alternative, so there's no point in beating my breast and wailing about it.' She sat down.

Heavy lids dropped over the golden eyes. 'How philosophical of you,' drawled Raoul.

'Yes, that's what I think,' Philippa agreed with composure.

'A great improvement.' There was a faint edge to the smooth voice, she thought. 'So you are resigned to marriage?'

She looked away across the still garden. 'On certain conditions, yes.'

'Conditions? But, of course,' he murmured.

She said on a little spurt of temper, 'Well, you must have expected me to discuss the terms of surrender.'

He put his head on one side. 'I don't think that is quite the way I would have put it,' Raoul drawled. 'But never mind. Go on with your conditons.'

She nodded. 'Well, to begin with I want to keep my independence,' she said briskly.

'In what form?' he sounded so relaxed he might be half asleep, she thought in indignation. She cast him a glance of dislike.

'I want to keep my job, for one thing.'

Raoul gave a soundless laugh. 'That is odd. That was going to be one of my conditions too.'

'Oh?' Philippa was astonished. He had said, though admittedly he did not know that she had understood, that her grasp of her job was unimpressive. Had he changed his mind? His next remark made it plain that he had not.

'I don't want you taking yourself off to Caverdons in a fit of pique.'

She bit her lip. 'I see,' she said chastened. 'Well, I can promise that I won't do that, I suppose. I would never have looked for a new job anyway except——'

'To get away from me?' he supplied. 'So now there will be no point in it. I am glad you see that. What other conditions?'

In spite of the fact that he was being so reasonable, Philippa began to feel nervous. She moistened dry lips.

'I want to keep my own flat,' she said, a touch of defiance creeping into her voice. 'To myself,' she added, as the smile began to curl his firm mouth. 'Private. As somewhere I can be my myself or entertain my friends if I want.'

Raoul considered it, sipping his coffee.

'You would not object that I should do the same thing?' he said at last.

Philippa stared at him. 'Of course not. I mean I would expect you to.'

'What an excellent, understanding wife you are going to make,' he mocked. 'How my friends will envy me. Any more conditions?'

Philippa swallowed. 'Divorce,' she said baldly.

The lids flew up and she saw that his eyes were blazing. She flinched back as if she had been unexpectedly impaled by a spear. He laughed again.

'Is it not a little premature to discuss divorce?'

She fought down a surprisingly strong instinct to back down. It was alarming that his anger should be so intimidating. Philippa realised that she would have to be very careful not to allow herself to be bullied by this arrogant man.

She said with very creditable calmness, however, 'I think we must accept that we are likely to have a separation at some point. These things can be unpleasant.' Her parents had talked about divorce often enough; they had always ended up screaming at each other about the sharing out of their possessions. 'I do not want to find that one tries to hold the other against their will.'

Raoul regarded her thoughtfully. 'Do you think that is likely?'

'Who knows? And I don't want us squabbling about the division of the spoils either,' Philippa went on hardily. She could sense the suppressed anger in him and ignored it. 'I keep my home and my salary and that is all I want when we split up.'

'I—see.' Raoul's face was unreadable. 'Well that disposes of two of the marriage vows, no perpetuity, no wordly goods. Would you like to suggest any other amendments?' The words bit. 'Do you want to discard the clause about forsaking all others, for example?'

Philippa shrugged. 'Naturally I didn't expect you'd want to be faithful to me as if I was a real wife. It never occurred to me.' She saw Shelley reappear round the side of the house with a tray. 'This looks like our breakfast.'

He ignored the rider. 'And now it has occurred to you?'

She kept her eyes on the approaching figure. 'What you do is your own affair,' she said distantly. 'As I said, I don't expect the privileges of a real wife.'

'You seem to be labouring under a misapprehension,

my dear,' Raoul told her expressionlessly. 'You are going to be a very real wife.' He stood up and looked down at her mockingly. 'And that is *my* condition.' He went towards the cook, relieving her of her tray with a charming smile, ignoring the blank dismay in Philippa's eyes.

Throughout that day and the next he refused to discuss the matter further. Philippa was therefore unable to extract from him either an explanation of his threatening remark or an assurance that it did not mean what she feared.

Instead, smiling dangerously, he remained at her side, holding her hand, stroking her cheek, dropping light kisses on her unprepared mouth whenever it seemed good to him. By the end of the day Philippa looked thoroughly rosy and confused, as if she were indeed the shy lover that Raoul was doing his best to imply.

As he conducted his campaign in the garden of the village pub, as well as at a swimming party, followed by dinner with friends, it was not surprising that the stares became less discreet and the comments more openly encouraging. Philippa, as she told him grumpily, felt as if she had been painted bright orange and hoisted from a flagpole.

It did, however, serve its purpose. There were paragraphs in two gossip columns on Monday morning to Raoul's evident satisfaction. And, more to the point, there was no reference to either Vivian Glass or Martin Industries on the financial pages. Philippa tried hard to think it had been worth it.

Raoul took her out every night. They went once to the theatre, twice to intimate little restaurants where, she suspected, he knew that journalists were likely to dine, and once to the opera.

The last outing was the only one she really enjoyed. Raoul was charming, when he wanted to be, a well informed conversationalist with a wit which kept Philippa in a constant ripple of appreciative amusement. But she never felt quite at ease with him. That faint hint of threat was always there. Whenever she tried to bring up the subject of their marriage he would smile that infuriating secret smile of his and tell her to stop worrying until it happened. As a result, of course, she worried all the more and the evenings in his company were undermined by that unresolved question mark.

But the opera was different. Philippa had always loved music, an inheritance from her father. It remained her great consolation for anxiety and pain.

He took her to Mozart. It was a hot night and the opera house was alive with the movement of fans. People who had come ill prepared fanned themselves with their programmes. None of this activity diverted Philippa from the action on stage or the exquisite intensity of the music. She was, temporarily, transfixed. Her worries fell away from her. Her slightly barbed verbal sparring with Raoul was forgotten. When the curtain fell on the final bars, she turned a face of absolute happiness to him.

'Thank you,' she said simply.

Raoul's smile was lop-sided. 'At least I have found one way to please you.'

The next day he put the notice of their engagement in the English and French papers.

After that events seemed to accelerate. Philippa was working as hard as she had ever done. It seemed as if, once Raoul was acknowledged as her future husband, customers who had previously seemed to hold back suddenly decided they had confidence in Vivian Glass and placed orders again. Some of the orders were big, in two cases for record amounts. Uncle David, delighted, began to talk of taking on more staff in the Shropshire factory once the merger itself was announced. Philippa, visiting customers up and down the country, and in constant meetings with the production managers, could only be grateful at the thought.

After the engagement was announced Raoul returned to France. He came back virtually every weekend, however, and drove Philippa down to the country. Once he had suggested that they stay in London but she had refused. The idea of spending the weekend hours with him on what she thought of as her own territory alarmed her. At least in the country his presence was to some extent neutralised by her aunt and uncle.

She had an uneasy feeling that Raoul knew the way she was thinking and was amused by it. When she had said firmly that she did not want to stay in London she had been certain of it.

'Why not?' he asked.

'Because—oh there's nothing to do in London at weekends,' Philippa said desperately.

The handsome mouth curled. 'You cannot be serious.'

'And it is such a waste of the fine weather to be cooped up in town.'

'There are parks,' he pointed out mildly.

'And anyway Aunt Margaret needs help with planning the wedding. Since you insist on such a large one,' Philippa ended triumphantly.

That at least was true. For his own unfathomable reasons, Raoul was determined on the textbook wedding in the village church with as many guests as the church could accommodate and the full panoply of flowers and wedding dresses and even—though Philippa had complained bitterly that it was a travesty—bridesmaids.

Her aunt, of course, was all in favour of these plans.

'You only get married once,' she remarked. 'Raoul is quite right. And it is very thoughtful of him to want you to have a day to remember. You will be grateful in years to come.'

Philippa doubted it very much but held her peace. She had not stipulated at the start that they would have a quiet register office wedding and did not think she was well placed to do so now. She had a strong feeling that she needed to hold her fire for more important battles.

She was almost sure that the element of display in the wedding on which Raoul was insisting was deliberate. It was as if he was setting his mark on her as publicly as possible. It frightened her whenever she thought about it. So, most of the time, she put it to the back of her mind.

She finally failed in her efforts to do so on the last weekend before the wedding. As usual they were staying with the Vivians and, again as usual, had been invited out to a dinner party in a neighbouring house on the Saturday evening. As soon as they walked into the party, Philippa recognised one of her fellow guests and stopped dead.

Behind her Rupert said maliciously, 'Oh good, Bob Sebastian is here. Haven't seen him for months. I'd heard he was in the States.'

Over her shoulder Philippa said in an even voice, 'Is this your doing, Rupert?'

They had entered ahead of the others. Aunt Margaret was exchanging greetings with an old friend; Raoul and David Vivian had been waylaid by a business associate. Rupert's voice was satisfied.

'Having him asked to dinner with the Breakspear's? Well, what do you think, sweet coz?'

'Why?' she cried softly.

He gave a harsh laugh. 'I thought that superior bastard could do with a shaking up.'

'Raoul? But what has it to do with Raoul? Don't you

see, you stupid creature, the only person who can be hurt by it is me?' Philippa told him in low voiced despair.

'You're a fool, Pipps,' Rupert told her in her ear. 'You used not to be. His money must have blinded you.'

And after that disturbing little interchange they did not manage to talk any more because their hostess surged over to greet them and they were sent off in different directions with instructions to 'circulate'.

It was a large party, with a barbecue grill set up in one corner of the garden. Their arrival had not been early and soon enough the grill was being lit among much merriment and a cheerful crowd gathered round it, armed with tongs and spatulas. Philippa knew most of the young people there. They had been schoolfriends and contemporaries of Rupert's, though one or two of them were acquaintances of her own.

She was talking to one such, a girl with whom she had once gone riding, when an arm was flung exuberantly round her waist and she was literally thrown off balance.

'Philippa Carr, you're still the most beautiful girl west of London,' said a slightly drunken voice. She was whirled round to find herself face to face with Bob Sebastian. 'And still look as if you've never been kissed,' he added, bending his head with unmistakeable intent.

Philippa pushed hard against him, her hands flat against his ribs, her spine curving painfully as she pulled against his hold.

For a horrifying moment, the years dissolved and Philippa was transported to another place where she had struggled in this man's arms. It was the night that his patience had finally run out, he said; the night he had made his grudging proposal of marriage. She was an anachronism, he had mocked, a Victorian miss in modern executive clothing. She always held him off, not because she did not want him, but out of some outdated idea that the bargain demanded a wedding ring, he had flung at her.

Very well then, he would marry her. He was too young, God knows, and he was probably being a fool. But he wanted her. And if that was the only way he could get her—and, provided of course, that David Vivian agreed to set them up in comfortable style—then he would, said Bob smiling, allow himself to be blackmailed.

Philippa had been stunned. For a moment she had not believed the evidence of her own ears. When she did, finally, assimilate the fact that Bob meant every light, insulting word, she had not cried or screamed at him. As a child she had learned to control her emotions in the face of disaster and she summoned all that skill to her aid. She thanked him, agreed with him that they were too young to marry and asked him, very quietly, to leave.

Whatever Bob Sebastian had expected to follow his proposal of marriage, it had not been that. He had obviously never even considered the possibility that he might be rejected and he flew into a rage. If he had not been so overwhelmingly furious, Philippa knew, he would never have resorted to violence. So she had been unprepared for the ugly look that came into his eyes and the even uglier intent with which he had flung himself upon her.

Looking at him now, seeing the spoilt child's charm and easy conscience which had permitted him to put all memory of that night out of his mind, she was rueful. For her it had been a horrifying awakening. She had thought herself in love, had always responded to his kisses with fervour, and yet, that night, she had been sick with distaste. She was frigid, he had flung at her bitterly. These days she was inclined to believe him. She had fought him off at the cost of no more than a few bruises and a grazed knuckle. She had persuaded him to leave her flat thereafter. She had never told anyone about the encounter. But it had left her as damaged as if she had achieved neither of those things and the whole world had been there to witness her humiliation.

Nor—until Raoul de Martin had issued that challenge and taken her body into his hands that night in France—had she felt any flicker of returning desire.

She said now in a troubled voice, 'Please, Bob, I——'

'Still don't like to admit you fancy me?' he said in drunken insolence.

She stepped sharply away from him, realising even as she did so that what he said would have been true at one time and now was so no longer. He did not begin to stir her pulses. But he did arouse her temper.

'Lay one finger on me and I'll scream,' Philippa told him crisply.

'There's no need to do that, my dear,' said another familiar voice.

Her wrist was abruptly released as Bob Sebastian found himself gazing up into eyes as yellow as those of a marmalade cat. Not a very well-disposed marmalade cat, thought Philippa suddenly.

'What the—who are you?' said Bob, focusing with evident difficulty.

Raoul took hold of Philippa's cold hand and held it in a vice.

'I am the man who is going to marry the lady you are annoying,' he said pleasantly.

There was a nasty silence. Then Bob said softly, 'Well, I'm damned.' He shot her a malevolent look and flung out a wavering hand in her direction 'Rather you than me, friend. I don't fancy dying of terminal frostbite.'

Raoul's hand tightened so sharply on her own that the bones cracked. Philippa winced; he did not appear to notice.

'How do you feel about a good hiding?' Raoul asked in a mild voice. So mild indeed that Philippa did not immediately understand the implied threat. But Bob Sebastian did. The blurred mouth curled back in a snarl.

'No need to take it out on me, sunshine,' he sneered. 'The only man *she's* ever wanted is her pretty cousin Rupert. Go and smash his face in, with my good will.

He lurched off. Philippa's hand was released. She flexed it carefully.

She said, trying to lighten the atmosphere, 'I never thought I'd hear you threaten physical violence. It doesn't go with your image, you know. Not at all cool.'

He shook the handsome golden head in mock sorrow. 'How little you understand me.'

But that touched a sore spot again. 'Yes,' said Philippa with a little shiver. 'Yes.'

She thought for a moment that he would have said more but they were interrupted by a laughing command from their hostess to Raoul to come and cook some food. Slightly to her surprise, because she did not think he was the sort of man who took kindly to orders, however lightly given, Raoul acquiesced.

Philippa watched him from a wooden seat under a trailing vine. In the light of the braziers and torches the fine profile was thrown into sharp relief. He turned his head, laughing at something the girl beside him had said and Philippa was assailed by an extraordinary sensation of pain.

He looked so completely at ease, at home among these party people, with his glamorous looks and all-encompassing sophistication. The girl who had made him laugh, a long legged blonde in shorts and striped T-shirt, was gazing at him with eyes just verging on the lustful. Philippa realised, with a stab, that for any woman in love with Raoul de Martin life would be a hell of jealousy. She was fortunate that she was not in love with him. She reminded herself of that a little desperately.

Oh, he was attractive enough; too attractive if she was honest. She was afraid of what might happen to her heart if one day she let down her guard and allowed herself to respond to his masculine appeal as that little blonde was avid to do. In other circumstances—if she had met him before she knew Bob Sebastian for instance—she might even have done just that. And then, thought Philippa grimly, where would she be? Fathoms deep in love with a man who did not want her and would have no trouble in attracting anyone he did want.

She shifted restlessly. What sort of woman would Raoul want, she asked herself, not for the first time. A sophisticate like himself—some perfectly groomed, sharp witted creature who staked no claims and sought no commitment? Probably. There had been plenty of people eager to tell her about the women that had preceded her in the gossip columns as the reported objects of his affection. Some were rich, all were beautiful. He would have no use for a plain working girl. So it was just as well that the plain working girl had no use for him.

She watched him joking with the blonde, unconscious of the wistfulness in her green eyes. But her expression hardened as he returned to her, bringing two plates of steak and salad and the adoring blonde. As they came closer, Philippa realised with a sinking heart that she even knew the girl. It was Sally Sebastian, Bob's sister.

'Hi, Pipps,' she said casually, flopping down on the grass and crossing her tanned bare legs with grace. 'I hadn't realised you were here until Raoul told me.'

Philippa looked from his face to hers and back. Sally Sebastian was an international jetsetter, just the sort of girl with whom, according to the gossips, Raoul was used to dealing.

'Do you know each other, then?' she asked in a polite little voice.

'You bet.' Years of city hopping had given Sally a faint transatlantic twang. 'I've been trying to do business with the man for the last twelve months. In fact, if it hadn't been for me he wouldn't have found you. It was me who sent him over to look at Vivian Glass, wasn't it, lover?' she added.

'Perhaps.' Raoul looked amused. He did not, Philippa noted, either respond to or repudiate the endearment. But when Sally leaned her shapely elbow on his knee he did not brush her away. 'You told me that you could get your scent bottles made cheaper and better in England. So I investigated.'

'You see?' Sally gave Philippa a friendly smile, unshadowed by any apparent consciousness of rivalry. 'So I guess I rate an invitation to the wedding.'

'Sally, you're impossible. You can't even hint in a ladylike fashion,' he complained with mock severity.

Sally turned a laughing pair of blue eyes up to him. 'Ladylike! Who's ladylike? When I want something I ask—otherwise how's the rest of the world going to know I want it? And if they don't know I want it, they don't give it to me.'

'And if they do, they do, I suppose. A refreshing philosophy, Sally,' Raoul said drily.

'Are you saying you disagree?' Sally was incredulous. 'Since when do you not say what you want—and go out after it like all hell, and get it?'

'Maybe.'

'Maybe nothing.' Sally appealed to Philippa, 'What do you say, Pipps? Isn't he the greatest go-getter you ever saw?'

'Raoul certainly seems to get what he wants,' Philippa said carefully, remembering with a little ache that he had once said the same of her and it had not been meant as a compliment. In order for it not to sound like an accusation therefore, she added hastily, 'Perhaps he's lucky.'

Raoul was watching her closely. She could feel his eyes though she did not look at him. He shook his head sorrowfully.

'How little you know me,' he murmured again.

And ran the tips of his fingers up her arm so that she shivered with a delicious chill at his touch.

Sally laughed good naturedly. 'He's certainly lucky if he's got you to marry him.' She turned to Raoul. 'It's always been something of a byword, Philippa's resistance to marriage. It would have to be an exceptional man to make her change her mind.'

The golden head, pale in the twilight, nodded slowly.

'So I am beginning to realise,' Raoul said in an odd voice.

Philippa wondered about that tone. Afterwards, when the dancing started and they were claimed by different partners, she could only give half her mind to the man with whom she was dancing. Why did Raoul sound like that? What did he mean? She was finding him more and more inscrutable.

She had hoped that as the wedding day approached, he would become more accessible, more willing to talk about his plans for the future. But the reverse had happened. Raoul became more remote every time she saw him. She felt that she understood him less and less. Oh the charm was still there, for her and for every other befuddled female that he honoured with his attention. He was courteous, considerate, even friendly in a distant fashion.

But underneath it all Philippa sensed that there was some emotion other than what he had allowed her to see. She thought of how he had threatened her on that first occasion they had met. He had never retracted his harsh words since. She had the feeling that he still despised her, in spite of his careful courtesy, and that once she was married to him she might well find him according her less than the slightly colourless consideration she was receiving from him at the moment. She was faintly alarmed at the prospect but exhilarated too. If Raoul de Martin thought he was marrying a woman whom he could start to bully the moment the ring was on her finger he was making a big mistake.

The party was a long one. The night air was as still as the day and almost as warm. Candles were guttering in their flowerpots by the time the first guests eventually began to leave. Philippa, who was strung up on the weeks of tension, was not tired and would have been glad enough to stay on and dance till dawn. But Raoul possessed himself of her hand and said a firm goodbye to their hosts.

'But Aunt Margaret and Uncle David are still here,' Philippa protested.

'They are not verging on collapse,' Raoul said crushingly. 'You look as if you are about to spontaneously combust. The sooner you get to bed the better.'

'But I shan't be able to sleep,' she returned like a sulky child.

He made no answer to that beyond an unsmiling look as he put her into the powerful car.

'Oh I suppose it's no use arguing with you,' she

complained and pulled the seat belt across her with quite unnecessary violence.

He did not speak on the short drive home. And when they arrived in front of the house Philippa bade him a stilted good night and slipped into the house and up to her room without waiting for his reply. If he decided that she was so tired she needed to go to bed at once, then he could jolly well make his own coffee, she thought vengefully. She knew that he always took coffee to his room where he worked after the rest of the household had retired. And she had seen the briefcase of papers that he had brought with him this weekend. So no doubt he would be working tonight. In fact their early departure from the barbecue was probably more for his benefit than her own.

Philippa undressed with angry movement. She had worked herself up into a rage which even the cool shower on her warm skin failed to modify. She opened all the windows in her room in the faint hope of catching whatever breeze there might be in the hot night. It was much too warm to wear anything in bed. She slid naked under the cool linen sheets and tried to compose herself for sleep.

As she had said to Raoul she was not really tired, though she knew quite well that after weeks of frenzied activity and tonight's party on top of it, she should be. She looked at the small carriage clock on her bedside table. It was half past two. With a small sound of frustration she turned on her side, pulling the pillows round her shoulders.

In the distance she became aware of a faint pattering noise. For a moment she hoped it was rain, and raised her head, but the air was as still as ever. The pattering came again, like a fall of pebbles dislodged on a beach. Philippa decided it must be one of the countless small noises that old houses made at night and subsided into the pillows again.

If she shut her eyes, perhaps she would doze. She must have drifted away from consciousness because she thought she heard someone calling her name. How odd, thought Philippa dreamily. Perhaps I will sleep tonight after all. Reassured, she began to relax.

Her state of dreamy well being was brought to an abrupt close by the unmistakeable slam of her window being crashed back on its hinges as far as it would go. Philippa came upright in bed with shock, her hand to her throat. A menacing figure, a creature out of a nightmare, met her eyes.

He was sitting astride the window sill, one leg already in the room and groping for a sure foothold. Philippa went cold. She suddenly realised that, apart from Raoul stationed by her wary aunt in the other wing, as far as possible from the supposed temptation of Philippa's bedroom, she was alone in the house. Desperately she realised there was no point in calling for help. A sob rose in her throat.

'If you scream,' said the intruder in a low, threatening voice, 'I shall probably fall off this damned narrow window sill.'

'*Raoul.*' She knew an instant's relief followed by a wave of fury. 'What the hell do you think you're doing?'

He balanced his hands on the wooden sill and threw his other leg over into the room. Then he jumped lightly down and, turning, put the window back on the bracket on which Philippa had left it.

He strolled over to the table which held her files and papers and calmly turned on the reading lamp before swivelling round to face her.

'Doing?' he said in a deceptively mild voice. 'Breaking and entering, of course, what do you think?'

'You terrified me,' Philippa flung at him.

Raoul gave a breathless laugh. 'A salutary experience for you. A little more terrifying in your formative years, and you might not have grown up to be a spoilt, self-centred brat.'

Philippa realised, with a chill of foreboding, that he was very angry indeed. But she refused to give way before it or to show her trepidation.

'How dare you speak to me like that?' she returned with no great originality but a fair amount of spirit. 'By what right . . .'

She was not allowed to finish.

'Right?' he blazed at her. '*Right? There* aren't any rights between you and me, Philippa Carr. We operate under the law of the jungle and you, for one, are never going to forget it.'

Before she knew what he was about, or had any inkling of what he intended, Raoul lunged across the room and took her shoulders hurtfully between his hard hands. Philippa saw his teeth gleam in a cruel, predator's smile. And then his mouth was on hers without pity.

When he had kissed her before he had not been kind but he had been in full control of himself. His object then had been to teach her a lesson. And he had done so. Now that negligent amusement had gone and with it all semblance of forbearance. He was quite simply furious and bent on wreaking his revenge on her.

What had caused this blind temper Philippa could not begin to guess. She tried to wrench her head away but in his passion he had lost none of that formidable strength and she was clamped between his hands as if they were the steel jaws of a trap. She was aching and gasping for breath when he finally released her. There was a taste of blood in her mouth, she did not know if it was his or her own, and the soft inner lip was swollen. She cupped both hands over her face like a hurt child.

'You shouldn't play rough if you don't like the consequences,' Raoul said in an unemotional voice, removing his hands and retreating to spindle legged chair under the window. He spun it round and swung himself across it staring at her sombrely. 'Don't ever try to take me on again,' he advised coolly. 'You'll regret it and it gets us nowhere.'

Philippa ran a forefinger along her tender lip, wincing slightly.

'I don't understand,' she said.

'No?' The cool voice mocked. 'You mean it was by accident that you dashed inside and slammed the door? That it was bad luck that you did not hear me call you to come and open the door? That you were so sleepy even stones thrown against your window couldn't wake you?' His voice roughened. 'Good God, you've been playing your tricks so long that you even believe in them yourself.'

Philippa shook her head slowly. 'I did think I heard my name called. But I thought I was drifting off to sleep. It never occurred to me it might be you.' She looked at him straightly. 'I think you owe me an apology.'

'Oh excellently done. That air of injured innocence is something special, do you know that?' he jeered softly. 'You're quite a lady. You lock me out; make me climb up a distinctly wobbly wistaria; scream at me when I arrive without breaking my neck; and then expect an apology.'

She gave a little laugh that broke in the middle. Her sore mouth was throbbing but she would not give him the satisfaction of seeing that he had hurt her.

'I didn't say I expected one. I know a lost cause when I see one,' she informed him. 'I said one was owing.'

Raoul's eyes narrowed. 'For a lady in your vulnerable position you are being very insulting,' he pointed out. 'Or don't you realise how vulnerable you are? Because your uncle approaches you on tiptoe and handles you with kid gloves, do you think I am going to do the same?'

She stared. 'I don't know what you're talking about.'

'Don't you?' He sank his chin in his crossed hands on top of the chair back and surveyed her. 'Well no, perhaps you don't. I suppose people are too embarrassed to say to you what they have been saying to me about you.'

Philippa flinched. 'What do you mean?'

Raoul's smile was wolfish. 'They say you're cold to the marrow of your bones. That you're only concerned about money and have wormed your way into the company so that you shan't be left without any.' He paused. Philippa said nothing. 'That you're frigid and are only interested in men you think can be of use to you,' he finished softly.

Philippa sat as if turned to stone. The ugly words crawled over her skin like insects. She felt sickened, infected, unclean.

She said numbly, 'You believe all that?'

Raoul shrugged. 'You haven't done a lot to disprove it, so far.'

She was stung. 'I agreed to marry you. That was surely not selfish?'

'You agreed to marry a millionaire who will save your career and your inheritance,' he said cynically. 'I don't think I'm flattering myself when I say the sacrifice is hardly enormous.'

It was odd, she thought remotely, that his words should hurt so much. After so many years of distancing herself from things that might hurt her, of disciplining herself not to feel the glancing blows of indifference, it was strange that a few malicious remarks from a man she hardly knew could hurt her so much she felt as if she wanted to die. The puzzled green eyes, dark with hurt, examined him, in his pool of light.

He was handsome. So were other men. So was her cousin Rupert with whom she had frequently squabbled and whose strictures she forgot at once. He was tough. So were most of the men she worked with and all the customers with whom she regularly did business. He had that devastating self assurance. Perhaps that was the trouble. He delivered his accusations with such absolute conviction that, although Philippa did not begin to recognise the character he painted as her own, she had no defences against him.

She put up a hand to shade her eyes.

'If you feel like that I don't see why you insist on this marriage.'

Raoul's expression tightened. She thought he was going to give her another lecture on her responsibilities to Vivian Glass and his own determination to support his company through thick and thin. But what he said was infinitely more disturbing.

'Don't you? Then you must be singularly unobservant.'

'Please,' her voice broke. She could not look at him. 'Please stop talking in riddles.'

'Very well.' There was an odd note in his voice. 'Let us say that you—intrigue—me. So cool, so composed. Look at you: even now you're not weeping and wringing your hands, are you? In spite of the fact that you made me very angry and you know that I am not likely to be pacified by any of the tricks that usually work. In spite of the fact that I have insulted you comprehensively.' He strolled across to her and took her chin between his fingers, turning her face up towards him. 'Not a tear, not a tremor.'

Philippa met his eyes squarely.

'Do you want me tearful and trembling?' she asked in a disdainful little voice.

The chiselled mouth curved; the heavy lids dropped over his eyes; the whole handsome face was unreadable.

'To be quite crude, my dear,' Raoul told her softly, 'I want you any way I can get you.'

His hands began to move as Philippa stared at him in undisguised horror. His spurt of laughter frightened her more than anything else in the whole incredible scene had done. She came out of her unnatural calm and struggled, pushing at him with all her strength. Raoul laughed again on a triumphant note and flung himself down beside her.

The sheet was utterly inadequate as protection and her struggles succeeded only in amusing him. He did not again kiss her bruised mouth but his lips laid a trail of fearful sensation down her throat and along the bones of her shoulder. It was so light she barely felt touched, so intense that she felt utterly changed by it into some new and exalted creature, trembling by a wing tip from the pinnacle of sensuality. She moaned a protest, as much at her own response as his humiliating skill.

'Hush,' he said, the words a breath against the pale skin of her breast.

And continued his slow, deliberate exploration of her every curve and bone and pulse point.

Gently, so gently she was hardly aware of it, the sheet was drawn away from her trembling body and discarded. The back of his hand caressed the soft flesh of her thigh in a touch as light as thistledown or falling leaves. Philippa began to shake, an urgent desire drumming in her blood. She wanted more than that teasing delicacy, that feather touch that mocked passion. Her body moved under his hand, yearning towards him.

Raoul made a sound in his throat like a satisfied tiger and she felt his teeth against the tender flesh of her inner elbow. His mouth travelled, his teeth closing on her skin in gentle bites that did not hurt and fuelled her need with their very restraint. Her spine arched and she reached for his shoulders, needing to halt that agonising seduction, to feel his whole body along the quivering length of her own.

Her hands were caught and held firmly to her sides. Unimpeded Raoul pursued his object. Philippa felt her nerves stretch tighter and tighter. Her body had a life of its own, was out of her control and would imminently take her to the heights of surrender. Her fingers moved under his. Her cheeks were wet.

'On no!' she begged him, hardly knowing what she said. 'No, please.'

He took no notice. She had not really hoped he would take any notice. Perhaps she did not even want him to. She was beyond thought or even self-protection. And as for Raoul, it seemed as if nothing could stop him taking her without compunction.

And then the door opened.

CHAPTER FIVE

THE scene that ensued haunted Philippa incessantly thereafter.

Margaret Vivian, anxious that her niece had looked tired and left the party early, had come to her room to check that she was not sleepless or unwell. The truth of the matter, though she did not admit this to her niece, to the offending Raoul, or even her troubled husband, was that she was very much afraid that Philippa would not go through with the marriage. And if she did not go through with it, reasoned Aunt Margaret, then Rupert's inheritance would be valueless, as the proposed merger would not go ahead. So she had intended to talk what she thought of as some sense into Philippa.

She had not bargained on finding her niece in bed with the very man that she seemed all set to jilt.

'Philippa!' she exclaimed, genuinely shocked. 'How could you?'

Raoul, as startled as Philippa but far more rapidly master of himself, raised his head.

'Did you knock?' he asked coolly.

Margaret Vivian flushed an unbecoming mottled shade. No, of course she had not knocked. She did not knock on doors in her own house. She had a right to enter any room she chose whenever she wanted. If people wanted to behave like animals they had no right to do it under her roof.

She continued at some length in this vein, her voice rising higher and higher, the baby blue eyes brimming with tears. Philippa tried so interrupt.

'Aunt Margaret,' she began, struggling up on her elbow.

71

But her aunt's gaze took in the naked shoulders and tumbled hair which told their tale too vividly. The childlike gaze was frankly horrified.

'Don't speak to me,' she wept. 'Don't you dare speak to me. You're unprincipled, disgusting. Oh, how could you do such a thing to me?'

Philippa flinched, clenching the sheet against her like a shield. Raoul gave her a swift, unsmiling look and swung himself off the bed, buttoning his shirt absently. Philippa averted her eyes, her hair swinging across her hot cheek. This was dreadful.

'You,' he said quite pleasantly to Margaret Vivian, 'are hysterical. I shall take you back to your room where you had better lie down.' He looked briefly back at Philippa, her arms hugged round her and her face hidden. 'I'll be back, darling,' he added casually.

Philippa's reaction was almost as fierce as her aunt's.

'No,' she ground out at exactly the same time as her aunt gave a little scream and launched into a tirade of which, mercifully, no more than one word in five was discernible.

Raoul laughed, a harsh sound, and took Margaret Vivian's elbow, steering her out of the room. As soon as they had gone Philippa darted out of bed and slammed and locked the door. She did not know whether he would really try to return to her, or whether he was simply being provocative in the face of her aunt's dismay, but she was not taking any chances. She had been too close, by far too close, to abject surrender.

She did not sleep for the rest of that night and so kept to her room in the morning in a not very successful attempt to rest. By the time she emerged Raoul had had to leave for France, Aunt Margaret said icily. He said he would call her. In future it would be better if Monsieur de Martin and Philippa confined their meetings to places outside the homes of decent folk. And Aunt Margaret did not speak to her again.

She did not keep it up, of course. Urged by her husband and her own unallayed fear that in the end Philippa might refuse to marry the man, Margaret Vivian flung herself into the preparations for the wedding and that meant of necessity that she had to talk to her niece. But the note of reproach was seldom absent when she did so.

Raoul, when Philippa desperately tried to talk to him, was unhelpful. Her aunt was a harridan, he said unsympathetically, and she was a goose to let it worry her. And he had no intention of releasing her from her promise.

Philippa was almost at the end of her tether when her cousin Rupert, noticing her pallor as they both left the office one night, suggested alluringly that he take her to his favourite bar and buy her a green demon.

Philippa smiled. 'What's a green demon?'

'My own invention. The recipe's a secret but I've taught it to Timmy at the Midnight Hour,' Rupert told her proudly. 'Though he's only supposed to make it for me and my guests. It is *bright* green.'

They made for the stairs, Rupert chatting lightly as if there was nothing on his mind other than cocktail recipes and the problems of parking a large car in the West End. But there were new lines round his eyes, Philippa noted shrewdly, and though the gaiety seemed unforced it did not quite banish the lingering shadow. Rupert was having to grow up fast, she thought compassionately.

In the bar they sat in enormous leather chairs and a jade green, faintly foaming, drink in a tall glass was put in front of her. Philippa regarded it with suspicion.

'What's in it?'

'Trade secret,' said Rupert nonchalantly, nibbling nuts.

'How does it taste?' pursued his cousin uneasily.

He grinned. 'Fairly foul. You don't drink it for the taste, you drink it for the style. *Il faut souffrir pour etre chic.*'

It tasted like washing-up liquid. Philippa told him so.

'Economy measure,' he responded wickedly. 'Give a girl one of these and she'll not want another. You've no idea how it keeps the bills down.'

The shadow touched his face again, as if he had reminded himself of something he would prefer to forget. He looked away.

'Bad time with bills, Rupert?' Philippa asked gently.

He shrugged. 'Bad time with accountants. The bills are quite civil in comparison. But those daily ledger merchants . . .!' He shuddered theatrically.

'But I thought they'd gone.' Philippa frowned.

'They have. They can still write though. Half my mail these days comes from the accountants or from Martin Industries. De Martin seems to be mounting a deliberate campaign against me.'

Rupert sounded weary. Because of this Philippa was impressed. She knew his temperament. Rupert would fire up in minute, get furious if anyone, as he put it, tried pushing him around. He was resentful of all control and volubly passionate on the subject. This weary resignation was something Philippa had not met from him before.

'Why should he do that?'

Rupert shrugged. 'I expect he wants me out. It can't be comfortable having the dispossessed heir at your elbow all the time.'

'But he has agreed——'

He gave her a wry look. 'Agreed what? To give me a job? Sure. He hasn't agreed to keep me if I'm an unsatisfactory employee. And he's obviously given his minions instructions to build up a dossier on me which shows that up to date I've given less than satisfaction in Vivian Glass. So when I start working for Vivian-Martin, I'll already have a record of misdemeanours. One more mistake and—exit Rupert Vivian.'

Philippa shivered. Rupert had a tendency to dramatise himself but in this case she was almost sure he was right. Raoul de Martin was not a man to leave anything to chance. He would make it very clear to Rupert that he was on probation and, if anything went wrong, would be dismissed. And the record was such, following the accountants' investigations, that Rupert would have no hope of legal redress.

'God, he's so calculating,' she said involuntarily.

Rupert glanced sideways at her in surprise.

'You've found that out too? But you're marrying him,' he reminded himself. 'I shouldn't talk to you like this about your future husband.'

'Talk to me any way you like,' Philippa begged him. 'At least it's real. Sometimes I feel as if I'm living in a nightmare and nobody will let me wake up.'

She spoke with vivid desperation. Rupert could see that Philippa was under considerable stress and she gave the impression of not having discussed it with anyone. He put a comforting arm round her shoulders, guiltily aware that he had been constantly hostile since the engagment was first mooted.

'No one can force you to marry him, Pipps,' he said soberly.

'No?' She gave a brittle laugh. 'That's not what Aunt Margaret thinks. And in my sensible moments I know it's the right thing. After all, we're both adults, both reasonably civilised people . . .'

Rupert interrupted her.

'If you think Raoul de Martin is civilised, you're nuts,' he said violently.

Recalling that Raoul himself had said it was the

law of the jungle between them, Philippa nodded slowly.

'But at least he won't beat me or lock me up,' she said, trying for flippancy. 'I can keep my independence.'

'He won't need to,' Rupert said with concentrated coldness. He looked at her pityingly. 'Come on, Pipps, where's your common sense? A man like that: he's played the field for fifteen years, I dare say. He knows how to get what he wants from a woman without beating her or locking her up. You won't stand a chance against him. You're too naïve. You'll be eating out of his hand before the honeymoon's over,' he concluded bitterly, 'and then you can wave goodbye to any independence you ever had.'

And that, thought Philippa, long after she had left Rupert and returned to her own comfortable flat, was true. She had not put up much of a fight in Paris, after all, nor on the night of the barbecue either. Raoul had found her little struggles amusing, she knew that, but he had not allowed them to stand in his way. If, for some inscrutable reason, he decided that he wanted a conventional marriage, with a devoted wife to warm his bed every night, she had little doubt that he would get it. She was already all too aware of his dangerous attraction. It would be so easy for him to enslave her physically; she knew quite well that any effort of will on her part would be powerless against the potent physical magnetism he possessed. And after physical defeat, what then?

Philippa buried her face in her hands. She could imagine it so clearly it was almost as if it had already happened. He would tire of her, become bored with her. Admit it, she told herself, you have little enough to offer him anyway. He is temporarily challenged by your resistance but once that it is overcome there will be nothing to hold his interest. And then you will be bereft, waiting in empty rooms for 'phones to ring or letters to arrive; trying to put together a career, a social life, as buffers against recurrent hurt. You have done it before.

And, she acknowledged, whatever Bob Sebastian had done to her heart and her self-confidence was as nothing compared with the devastation that Raoul de Martin had the power to wreak. She approached her wedding day in a state of growing panic that was all the more profound for being unexpressed.

It did not, however mar the perfection of the wedding. A bride was expected to be pale. If the dark green eyes looked too big for the white face, it was put down to over-excitement. Nobody, except perhaps the groom, observed the look of lingering horror. Philippa herself thought she looked like a frightened child abandoned in the dark and did her best to hide it.

There were, admittedly, one or two of Aunt Margaret's friends who observed that she had lost weight and took her to task over it. But they ascribed her thinness to over-enthusiastic dieting before the wedding. They even envied her a little, those stout matrons in their smart outfits with their happy marriages to return to after the reception. They wished they could lose weight so easily. Though of course dear Philippa had not needed to and it would be dangerous if she allowed herself to get too thin.

Philippa did not tell them that she had made no effort at all to diet. The effort had been involved in eating, if anything. She had completely lost her appetite, while she was living on excess energy, going like a bat out of hell all day, as her cousin Rupert put it, and collapsing into disturbed sleep at night.

As a result she looked not only thin and pale, but tense as whipcord, the enormous green eyes sparkling, the long beautiful hands restless. And her mouth, as again only the groom noticed, prevented from trembling only by immense self control. The schooled lips smiled, uttered platitudes, kissed scented cheeks. The despair could be detected only occasionally when she thought herself unobserved and the rigorously repressed pain compressed the corners of the sweet mouth.

But everyone agreed that she was a beautiful bride. Some of them were rather surprised to admit it. Philippa was well liked and she was known to be a stylish girl in her way but she lacked, as the vicar put it to his wife, that softness that made a bride look truly beautiful. But in flowing ivory paper taffeta, with a cobweb of lace veil on her soft and shining hair, and a trailing bouquet of country flowers from her uncle's garden, she was exquisite. She even, to the vicar's immense satisfaction, had a tearful moment when, on leaving the vestry, the bridal party had begun its progress down the altar to the strains of a Bach chorale.

The vicar had been against Bach. Too chilly for a wedding, he said, too ascetic. But the bridegroom had insisted. And certainly little Philippa seemed moved by it. The vicar sighed sentimentally. It seemed that the bridegroom knew what he was about after all.

For Philippa herself, that moment of emotion at the altar steps had been frightening. She knew she was very near the limits of her endurance. She could not bear it if she were to break down in the middle of all the rejoicing.

So she stiffened her resolve, took several deep breaths, and passed the rest of the afternoon with her fortitude tried severely but never overcome. By the time she was motioned away to change for departure by her aunt, she was almost drunk with the effort of pretence.

Looking at her over-bright eyes her aunt said doubtfully, 'You haven't had too much champagne, have you dear? It's very warm outside. It could have gone to your head.'

But Philippa laughed. She had drunk little and eaten less. She felt light headed and reckless.

'Shall I tell Raoul that you ought to have a little rest before you leave?' pursued Aunt Margaret, growing more worried by the minute.

'Don't bother. I can sleep in the car,' said Philippa indifferently.

She was as good as her word and Raoul did not try to prevent her. After one assessing look, he had handed her into the long low car, now playfully daubed with confetti and slogans, and solemnly buckled her into her safety harness. Then he had kissed her mouth for good measure. There was a loud cheer from the assembled guests and Philippa smiled, stretching her lips in one last meaningless gesture for the world's benefit. Then, as they turned out of the drive on to the quiet road, she slid down into the upholstered comfort of the seat, slipped her hand under her cheek, and slept.

It was not a journey she could ever afterwards remember very clearly. She knew that it was very hot outside and could recall Raoul solicitously adjusting the air conditioning and the sunshield so that she should be comfortable. She remembered his soft laugh as she slumped drowsily back against the seat after a humpedback bridge had sent her stomach spiralling.

She thought that she remembered also being carried to an aeroplane; even that she could recall the touch of his hands as he fastened the seat belt. In her drowsy state, the mundane gesture had seemed oddly tender and, for an instant she had had the illusion of being cared for. It was strangely disquieting. And it moved her.

And then, when they arrived in France and she tried groggily to rouse herself, she found that she was eavesdropping involuntarily again. I really must tell him that I speak French, she thought muzzily. And soon.

She was not sure who was speaking. They were at some distance from her in the airport lounge. Raoul had gone to see about the car that was supposed to be waiting for them. Clearly he was well known at the airport.

'So he has been broken to bridle at last,' one of them said, sounding amused.

'By the pale English girl?' said the other scornfully. 'Be your age.'

'But she is attractive. Surely he is in love with her.'

'Attractive! Pouf! She could be beautiful if she wanted. And she does not want,' said the unknown Frenchman shrewdly. 'She will not be allowed to interfere with Monsieur's activities, my friend; take my word for it.'

Philippa, feeling as if she had inhaled ashes, shut her eyes tight and pretended to be fast asleep when Raoul returned.

CHAPTER SIX

THE house at which they eventually arrived was, as Philippa told him wryly, the closest thing to a royal fortress she had ever entered.

Raoul grinned at her. 'It's a simple country gentleman's house,' he protested. 'It's just that in this part of Aquitaine a country gentleman's life was a bit precarious. Usually,' he added, 'because the English were invading at the time. Hence the battlements. But you'll find it quite comfortable.'

And that, she found, was an understatement.

They were greeted at the side door into a fortified courtyard by a small sprightly man wearing a baize apron.

'Gerard,' said Raoul briefly. 'He speaks English. You won't have any trouble.'

Philippa cast him a doubtful look, as her conscience stirred again. But Gerard, beaming from ear to ear, was shaking her hand enthusiastically.

'Madame, at last. Such a great pleasure. Such a very great pleasure.' He seized their cases from the boot of the car with a flourish and, still talking, trotted ahead of them into the stone flagged hall. 'Wonderful day, wonderful weather. There will be a splendid sunset to welcome you, Madame. We are famous for our sunsets. And, Monsieur, I regret but they have been telephoning from Paris.'

Raoul nodded as if he were not surprised by the news.

'Would you ask Henriette to show my wife to her room,' he said. 'And take the cases up. I'll go to the study and get these messages dealt with now.'

How casually he said it, marvelled Philippa, shocked to hear herself identified as his wife. She put a hand to her throat to ease her suddenly constricted breathing. If only she could relax; if only she were not so aware of him all the time. If only she were not so afraid.

Her thoughts were interrupted by the arrival of the housekeeper.

'Madame la Comtesse,' she greeted her formally, giving Philippa another bad moment, 'it is good you are here.'

Henriette Longine was no taller than her husband but she was twice as round, a comfortable butterball of a woman with warm brown eyes, clearly bent on welcoming Philippa to the château with all the warmth of which she was capable. And a good deal of pride as well. She flung open the doors of the main apartment.

'We have been in preparation for so many weeks,' she said simply. 'I thought Monsieur would never be satisfied.'

Philippa looked about her in amazement. It was a high-ceilinged room built on the corner of the edifice so that it had the benefit of deep windows on two sides. The walls were hung with tapestries, only the muted colours bearing witness to their great age. The floor was of wood, waxed and polished until it shone like a chestnut mirror. It was covered with woven rugs which, Philippa's discerning eye told her, were as fine as the tapestries.

The whole was dominated by a fourposter bed the size of a small barge. It was hung with heavily embroidered curtains that at the moment were looped back and tied to the twirled and twisted bedposts. Philippa stared at it, whitening. She felt as she sometimes did in the ancient lift at Vivian Glass when it suddenly lurched into action unexpectedly: as if she had lost her stomach. She had never seen a piece of furniture that was more emphatically, more self-consciously, a '*lit matrimonial*'.

Henriette seemed unaware of her dismay.

'And this is Monsieur's dressing room,' she said chattily, opening double panelled doors.

Philippa considered it in silence: a desk, a couple of chairs, wardrobes, chests of drawers and, though unpostered and uncurtained, a substantial bed. She drew a breath of relief. Until that moment she had not been quite sure of Raoul's good faith, she realised.

'And Madame's sitting room,' ended Henriette triumphantly, traversing the room and flinging open the doors on what struck Philippa as a bower of roses.

She stopped dead, startled. The room had obviously been newly decorated in shades of emerald and sea blue with touches of ivory. And on every window ledge and polished table—even on the bookcase—were bowls of ivory roses.

The room was full of their heady perfume. Philippa was deeply touched.

'Oh, Henriette,' she said breathing it in. 'It is wonderful. How can I ever thank you?'

Henriette looked complacent but faintly surprised. 'I merely carried out Monsieur's orders,' she said. 'He will be glad you are pleased.'

'I must tell him,' said Philippa warmly, though she in her turn was surprised. Nothing she had ever heard about or experienced of Raoul de Martin would have led her to expect so imaginative a gesture.

She did not say as much when she thanked him but nevertheless she must have betrayed it because his look was wry.

'Did you think I would be less attentive than that fellow Sebastian?'

Philippa jumped. She had not mentioned Bob to Raoul. She frowned.

'He used to deluge you with flowers, did he not? At least that's what his sister tells me,' he went on in a barbed voice.

It was not entirely untrue. In the beginning, when he first started in pursuit, Bob had sent her daily bouquets. They had been delivered by the florists on the corner and Philippa was fairly certain that Bob had never had the slightest idea or interest in what blooms they contained.

She said carefully, 'That was different.'

Raoul was ironic. 'Because you were not married to him? But some people have to do their wooing after marriage.'

She said nervously, 'Raoul . . .'

But he interrupted. 'The roses came from our own rose garden which is very old. You will find this area is famous for its flowers as well as its sunsets. Which by the way, we had better inspect closely or Gerard will be disappointed.'

He poured wine into two fluted glasses, handed one to her and gestured imperiously to the windows that looked out over the darkened terrace to the landscape beyond.

The sunset was spectacular; as was the meal, served to them on the terrace by the beaming Gerard, which followed. Philippa said so and Raoul smiled.

'You must tell Henriette. She will be triumphant. Normally when there are guests I tell her to hire a chef and she gets very indignant.'

Philippa gave a great sigh of satisfaction.

'I don't know why you bother. I've never had such a superb meal.'

Raoul laughed. 'You don't yet know how large the château is. Gerard and Henriette run it with a certain amount of help from the village. And of course there are resident gardeners. But there is plenty for Henriette to do when there is a houseparty without cooking three meals a day for twenty or thirty people as well.' He sipped his wine. 'Of course if you like it and want us to spend more time here, we shall have to increase the permanent staff.'

It hung in the air between them: a question about more than the château's housekeeping arrangements. Philippa looked away.

'Raoul,' she said with difficulty, 'I don't want—I mean it is not part of our bargain that you should alter your life in any way for me.'

His smile was a little twisted. 'How much greater alteration can there be than marriage?'

'But it need not be,' said Philippa. She added helplessly, 'Oh, can't you see what I'm trying to say?'

'Yes.'

Nothing more than that; just an affirmative in a clipped voice. The casual friendliness was gone. Philippa dared one swift look at him and averted her eyes. He looked harsh, remote, the fine bones of his face etched by the candlelight to an implacable mask.

She did not understand, she thought in despair. Sometimes he seemed indifferent, even careless about this strange union of theirs. At others she had the feeling that his plans regarding their marriage, though private from her, were very precise. But whenever she tried to talk to him about it he either froze up or changed the subject.

And of course her own bewildering range of feelings did not help. There was marriage, with its overtones of invasion, which she had always feared. Her parents had made a prison of it for each other and Philippa knew she could never forget that. She had a deep, superstitious feeling that marriage would make of her, too, both a prisoner and a gaoler. Had she not already felt that humiliating stab of jealousy, when Raoul was talking to charming Sally Sebastian? If she allowed herself to be seduced into making this marriage a real one, how many and how frequent would those pangs of jealousy become?

She shook her head involuntarily at her thoughts, not realising that she had moved. Nor did she realise that the man across the table from her was watching her minutely, noting every fleeting expression. She bit her lip.

If she was honest, Philippa told herself, it was not just marriage in general that she was afraid of, any more than it was the fear of physical mishandling. Bob Sebastian had been brutal, and she could not remember that encounter without a shudder, but she did not make the mistake of thinking Raoul would use violence in making love to her. Indeed, she had already experienced that devastating physical competence with which he had reduced her to ardent compliance.

No, what she feared was the power that Raoul would have over her if she let him approach too close. He had called her cool and a lot of people who knew her thought she was unemotional. But Philippa, though she could put on an excellent act for others, knew herself better than that. She did not love easily but when she did she loved for ever. If she permitted herself to love Raoul she would put into those charming hands a weapon which could destroy her.

She said quietly, 'I think we have to look on this marriage as something purely temporary; an unfortunate interlude. We must try to see to it that it makes as little difference as possible to the ordinary conduct of our lives.'

The candles, lit by the romantic Gerard, were guttering. There was no electric light and the shadows flickered wildly. Raoul looked as if he were in bitter pain but that must be, thought Philippa, the effect of the wavering shadows.

'That is really your preferred solution?' His voice was perfectly composed.

She faced him squarely. 'It is.'

'You are an intelligent woman. You have no doubt considered the option of our marriage being——' he paused and then said with some care '—more than temporary.'

'It is not a real option, I think,' said Philippa sadly.

'May I know why?'

She spread her hands. 'Us,' she said simply. 'The people we are.'

'You are so certain that we are incompatible?' he asked curiously.

'Oh come on, Raoul,' Philippa flashed. This conversation was oddly painful. She had a tiny suspicion that he was setting out to dig under her skin. 'You've been very civil today and I'm grateful for it. But most of the time we verge on being enemies. You must know that as well as I do.'

Four of the candles had died. Two more now flared up and subsided leaving them in almost complete darkness. Philippa could see the little flame of the last candle reflected in his eyes. It burned steadily.

'But surely you must also know that there is hostility and hostility,' Raoul murmured, amusement plain in his voice. 'You are not without experience.'

'My experience,' Philippa told him steadily, 'tells me that when two people of totally opposing tastes and temperaments get married, they had better not expect it to last. We have the advantage of admitting that from the start. So we may perhaps avoid being hurt.'

'How clever of us,' said the smooth voice. 'But I think it would take something more than a failed marriage to hurt a little icicle like you. If you really mean what you say, I do not think you are in danger, my dear.'

'I mean what I say.' Philippa could hardly say the words, her throat was so taut. Her heart was pounding furiously, so that she thought he must hear it.

It horrified her. He was, after all, offering her nothing. He had, in veiled terms, suggested that they ignore the implicit conditions on which she had entered into this marriage but he had not said why. No doubt he thought it was wasteful not to take what pleasure they could out of the arrangement.

But Philippa, knowing the price she would have to pay for that pleasure and suspecting by the minute that it would be infinitely greater than she had ever realised could be possible, was not to be tempted.

'I mean what I say,' she repeated hardily.

He gave a faint, very French shrug. She saw his shoulders move against the pale horizon to be seen through the window.

'Then there is no more to be said.'

Philippa sagged against the back of her chair. She had been taut as if braced for battle. Now, she supposed, she had won. It made her feel desolate. Now that it was too late she wished she could recall her words. But it would not have been wise. Better to leave things as they were.

'Shall I ring for more candles?' Raoul asked with remote courtesy.

Philippa shook her head, 'No, don't bother for me. I'm very tired. I think I'll go to bed now.'

She was grateful that she could make that statement without any undertone of apprehension. Since seeing the bed in Raoul's dressing room she had been quite clear that he was not intending to join her tonight. Perhaps he would have done so had she responded to his overtures this evening. But, for better or worse, she thought wryly, she had made it plain that she wanted to keep a distance between them. And he had not over-persuaded her or indeed seemed either surprised or much disappointed at her decision.

No, Philippa thought, she could sleep alone and undisturbed without any fear of Raoul invading her privacy. He was much too civilised and subtle for that. Unconsciously, she sighed.

If he heard her, he did not refer to it. He rose to his feet courteously as she stood up.

'I'll say good night then,' she said a little awkwardly.

Should she shake hands? Offer a kiss? He did not help, standing there in the light of one candle in enigmatic silence. She pushed back her chair. It scraped along the polished floor, loud in the quiet room.

Raoul moved but only to open the door for her. Outside a dim light was burning on the staircase.

As her eyes grew accustomed to it Philippa turned to him, wanting to say something to restore their previous friendliness. But it was impossible. His face was closed, his eyes unreadable.

But as she hesitated he reached out and took her hand. And, to her startled amazement, turned it over and pressed a very soft kiss into the palm. Then, without a word, he went back into the dining room and shut the door on her.

Philippa made her way upstairs slowly, in a daze, that infinitesimal pressure seeming to burn the bones of her hand still. She carried the hand to her cheek. If only he had not done that. If only he were not the complicated sophisticate that he was. If only she had more self-confidence or more strength to resist him. If only—she went into her room on trembling legs and undressed as if in a dream—Raoul were not so diabolically attractive.

In spite of the tension of the day Philippa slept

almost at once. The bed intimidated her a little at first
but when she had pushed back its heavy coverlet and
stripped the rest of the bedclothes down to the simple
sheet which was all she could bear in the heat, it looked
less like an antique monument.

She had brought with her a simple white smock,
embroidered with flowers at the neck and the mid-thigh
hem. It was cotton, cut away widely from throat and
arms and was the coolest thing she had found to sleep
in. The high bedroom, presumably because the shutters
had been kept closed all day, was considerably cooler
than her room in the Shropshire house or her London
flat.

Leaving the shutters and windows wide to the night
air, she crept between the exquisitely pressed and
scented linen and slept.

She had already had a dream, a dark thing of vague
demons, when she was awoken. At first she lay still, her
heart beating hard, not knowing where she was or what
had woken her. Then she made out the silhouette of a
chaise longue against the sky and, turning her head, saw
the windows on the other outside wall open on to the
balcony. From them came the scent of wallflowers.

It was now dark night. The sky at both windows was
the colour of blue black velvet, studded with tiny
diamond points of stars. For a moment Philippa had
the dazed sensation that she was riding in a chariot
across the expanse of sky. Then, clearing her head with
a little shake, she pulled herself up on her elbow,
looking about her in the shadows.

What had woken her? She had not been reading;
there was no book left carelessly on the bedside table to
fall in the night and disturb her. The servants slept in
their own quarters above the kitchen; they could not
possibly have woken her up. Was it Raoul, going to bed,
making unfamiliar noises that had broken her sleep?

She looked across to the doors that led to his dressing room. There was no sliver of light underneath to reveal whether he was up and awake. And then, as her eyes accustomed themselves to the blackness of that corner of her room, she went rigid.

For the doors were not, as she had thought, closed but stood wide open. And leaning against the door jamb, one foot negligently crossed over the other, stood the husband to whom she had already, so decisively, wished good night. Philippa's blood seemed to freeze in her veins.

Raoul was smoking. She registered that with some surprise, in spite of her alarm. She could not recall seeing him smoke before, except a cheroot after dinner. Now the faint glow and fade of the cigarette was the principal sign of his presence.

He seemed to be staring at the bed without moving. For a moment Philippa hoped that he might not have realised that she was awake. But then she saw that she had been too unguarded in her awakening. He could not have missed the small movements. And probably, in spite of the masking curtains, he had seen her move up on to her elbow.

Her mouth was dry. She tried to speak and nothing came. It was like the continuation of her nightmare. Only now the demon was not vague: he wore a pale shirt and smoked and stared at her out of the darkness.

'Raoul?' It was little more than a squeak, she thought dismayed.

The powerful shoulders shifted, left the door frame. Unspeaking he crossed to her, silent-footed and menacing as a ghost.

Her voice rose in panic. 'Raoul, what are you doing here?'

A low, predator's chuckle was her only answer. The sheet, which in her disturbed sleep she had twisted and pulled awry, was ripped away and tossed to the end of the bed. There was something uncontrolled about the movement, a fury verging on violence in that one simple action, which reminded her horribly of another, colder, night in London and another angry man.

'Raoul.' She was pleading with him, her voice, her whole body suppliant. 'What do you want?'

He did speak then, jeeringly. 'Do you really need me to tell you?'

Raoul took hold of her upper arms and jerked her forward so that she was brought tumbling to her knees on the bed facing him, gasping with shock.

'I want you,' he said coldly. 'I told you that before. And I'm having you. It is—you may recall—part of the marriage contract.'

She was almost weeping, pulling frantically away from him.

'But we had an understanding, we agreed . . .'

'I,' he said, in that still, dead voice, 'agreed to nothing. You dictated a few conditions but—again if you recall—I never agreed to them. As far as I'm concerned you pledged what you promised in church. And I don't intend to settle for anything less.'

'Oh God!' It was a faint exclamation of pure fear. 'You can't do this.'

'A bargain is a bargain, my dear.'

'Bargain!' Philippa winced from the cold word as if it were a blow. 'What sort of man *are* you, Raoul de Martin? Don't you know that you can't bargain over people?'

'I am the sort of man who collects my debts. Nobody cheats me, little one, not even long-legged schoolgirls with big eyes and calculating little minds.'

'Cheat! Bargain! I think you're out of your mind,' said Philippa fervently. 'I'm not a commodity, for God's sake. I'm a woman.'

Raoul's hands tightened cruelly on the soft flesh of her arms.

'You are indeed,' he agreed silkily. 'A woman whose intelligence I rate highly. A woman who used that intelligence to decide in favour of marriage. Now, I don't know whether you thought you could talk me into observing those conditions of yours after we were married. Or if you are not as keen on the idea of—er— separate development—as you pretend. Maybe all these maidenly struggles are as big a sham as everything else about you.' His teeth gleamed in a smile without humour or kindness. 'Let's find out, shall we?' he said quite gently.

Philippa closed her eyes. She had not fought with anyone physically since she was a child. She could not now bring herself to bite and claw and scratch as she had done then. And yet there was no other way to defend herself. She raised a wavering hand which he captured easily and used to pull her hard against his body. Her head was wrenched back and her hair, which she had pinned up off the back of her neck for coolness, escaped its pins and tumbled down to flow over her shoulders and breasts like liquid shadow.

She was breathing fast and shallowly. Raoul bent, very slowly, curving her back until she thought her spine would break and then set his mouth against the exposed length of her slim throat. Philippa tried to free herself but it was hopeless. She was off balance, her hands imprisoned behind her, and no match for his strength. The cotton shift was disposed of with contemptuous ease and he set, inexorably, about the task of reducing her body to frenzy.

The last time he had subjected her to deliberate, tantalising patience, as if determined to wring the last drop of response out of her. Tonight there was no pretence of any such thing. He would not, it was clear, brook any delay at all. The powerful hands disposed her without even token courtesy.

'No!' she said hoarsely, helplessly.

Raoul ignored her. It was like that terrible struggle with Bob Sebastian. Philippa began to shake convulsively. Bob had been brutal in his anger. Though she had, eventually, managed to wriggle away and lock herself in the bathroom before he completed his design, she had ever since had a horror of finding herself in exactly this position, pinned and helpless in the face of a sexual onslaught which sickened her.

She lost all sense of time and place. She forgot completely that this was Raoul to whom she had, only that evening, been acknowledging to herself that she was more than attracted. She writhed against him, desperate to escape.

'Let me go,' she begged, all sense of dignity lost in her terror. 'For the love of God, let me go.'

Raoul did not even seem to hear her. He was completely absorbed, his hands, his mouth tolerating no denial, exploring every inch of her body. She was cold as ice, shaking uncontrollably, and where his lips moved Philippa felt scalded. Locked in her fear, she was incapable of response. But she did not beg for her freedom again. She lay rigidly silent.

Raoul could not ignore that rigidity. He raised his head and stared into her eyes in the darkness.

'Philippa,' he said, a note in his voice that might almost have been pleading.

But a torturer does not plead with his victim, though Philippa bitterly.

She said with the calm of despair, 'If you do this I'll hate you for ever.'

He brushed the hair off her shoulder with hands that shook slightly.

'It doesn't have to be hate,' Raoul told her in an

urgent undervoice. He took her face between his hands, touching his tongue gently to her lower lip.

Philippa closed her eyes. 'What else can it be?' she demanded stonily.

Raoul went very still. Then he said very quietly, almost under his breath, 'Damn you.'

And unleashed on her the full force of his pent-up need. He made no allowance for her innocence, for the fragility of her body compared with his own, or for her palpable fear. He used her with a strength that made her wince and yet took her far out into space, so that she was hurtling through the midnight air among the stars, guided and held steady by those wickedly accomplished hands. And then she was pierced to the heart by pain so unexpected that she had not even attempted to brace herself against it.

There was an ugly, truncated gasp of agony which she recognised dimly as her own. And then she was falling, headlong out of the sky and into a dark pit where pain ended and oblivion consumed her.

CHAPTER SEVEN

PHILIPPA woke late and alone. The sun was streaming in between the open shutters and the distant fields shimmered in the mid-morning heat. The pillows were wildly tumbled but somebody, presumably Raoul, had drawn the sheet up over her body.

She sat bolt upright and pressed her hands to her burning cheeks. She could not face him. Her humiliation last night had been total. She did not think she could bear to see him again.

There was a soft tap on the door to the corridor. Philippa jumped, looked at it warily. But Raoul, she thought shivering, would not knock on the door. He had stated last night what he believed his rights to be and she had no doubt that they included the right to enter his wife's bedroom without permission whenever it took his arrogant fancy. So she plucked up her courage and called out, 'Come in'.

It was Henriette, beaming.

'Madame has rested well?' She had a tray in her hands, bearing a steaming bowl of coffee and a vase containing a single ivory rose. 'Monsieur said that you would be tired after so much travelling and to leave you to sleep.'

Philippa's face was delicately tinged with colour but there was no salacious undertone to Henriette's words. The housekeeper met her eyes frankly.

'Monsieur himself has been working,' she informed Philippa with a tinge of disapproval. 'But now he has finished and Gerard has taken the papers to the post and Monsieur is swimming.'

TO EXPERIENCE A WORLD OF ROMANCE.

How to Enter Sweepstakes & How to get 4 FREE BOOKS, A FREE TOTE BAG and A BONUS MYSTERY GIFT.

1. Check ONLY ONE OPTION BELOW.
2. Detach Official Entry Form and affix proper postage.
3. Mail Sweepstakes Entry Form before the deadline date in the rules.

H·A·R·L·E·Q·U·I·N
FIRST·CLASS
Sweepstakes

OFFICIAL ENTRY FORM

Check one:

☐ Yes. Enter me in the Harlequin First Class Sweepstakes and send me 4 FREE HARLEQUIN PRESENTS® novels plus a FREE Tote Bag and a BONUS Mystery Gift. Then send me 8 brand new HARLEQUIN PRESENTS® novels every month as they come off the presses. Bill me at the low price of $1.75 each (a savings of $0.20 off the retail price). There are no shipping, handling or other hidden charges. I understand that the 4 Free Books, Tote Bag and Mystery Gift are mine to keep with <u>no obligation to buy.</u>

☐ No. I don't want to receive the Four Free HARLEQUIN PRESENTS® novels, a Free Tote Bag and a Bonus Gift. However, I <u>do</u> wish to enter the sweepstakes. Please notify me if I win.

See back of book for official rules and regulations.   108-CIP-CAJ4
Detach, affix postage and mail Official Entry Form today!

FIRST NAME_____ LAST NAME_____
                           (Please Print)

ADDRESS_____ APT._____

CITY_____

PROV./STATE_____ POSTAL CODE/ZIP_____
"Subscription Offer limited to one per household and not valid to current Harlequin Presents® subscribers. Prices subject to change."

ENTER THE H•A•R•L•E•Q•U•I•N

FIRST•CLASS *Sweepstakes*

Detach, Affix Postage and Mail Today!

Harlequin First Class Sweepstakes
P.O. Box 52010
Phoenix, AZ 85072-9987

Philippa reached gratefully for the coffee, tucking the sheet securely under her arms.

'Swimming?' she echoed in surprise. 'I did not realise we were near the sea?'

'Oh no, not the sea.' Henriette was dusting the little table under the oval mirror with a corner of her apron, moving the ornaments on it to her satisfaction. 'But there is a pool. Monsieur had it put in when he inherited.'

She bent to inspect a mark on the linen sheet, frowning. Philippa tensed. Henriette shook her had disapprovingly.

'That Monsieur Raoul,' she said, clicking her tongue. 'One of these days he will burn us all in our beds,' and she exhibited for Philippa's condemnation a small burnt hole in the fine material.

Philippa flushed and buried her nose in her coffee cup. Memory stabbed her. He had been smoking last night as he stood there in silence watching her; like some underworld villain lounging in a doorway, waiting for the right moment to embark on his crime. And then he had plundered.

Seeing her white face and mistaking the cause, Henriette said comfortingly, 'It is only when he is disturbed that he smokes, madame. When things do not go well with the business. And that will all change now, so Monsieur says.'

She went out eventually, taking the tray with her, leaving Philippa to bath and dress in the clothes she had laid out for her. The soft muslin blouse and floaty skirt looked, thought Philippa wryly, a little impoverished when artistically disposed on green velvet upholstery.

They looked even more impoverished by the elegant swimming pool. Raoul was stretched out on a bleached willow lounger with his head back. And at that angle his face looked taut, almost unhappy. Philippa paused in the archway of the wall which surrounded the pool area. She felt awkward and off balance. But she was no coward, so she straightened her shoulders and walked towards him, skirting tubs of multi-coloured geraniums.

He lifted his head and watched her unsmilingly. Her nervousness increased.

'Are you all right?' he demanded abruptly.

She could not pretend that she did not know what he was talking about, though she flushed at the downright question.

'Of course.'

'There is no of course about it,' he told her. 'I have never seen a woman as frightened as you were last night.'

She swallowed. This was getting too close to private territory. She must deflect him before he started to probe deeper. She must lighten the tone.

So she seated herself composedly in the chair next to his and gave him the best smile she could manage.

'Well, what can you expect? Henriette says I was lucky not to be burned in my bed.'

He looked at her in frowning enquiry.

'She obviously disapproves of your habit of smoking in bedrooms,' Philippa explained.

Raoul was impatient. 'I dare say, but what I want to know ...'

'You burnt the sheet last night,' Philippa interrupted hastily.

There was a little silence. Raoul looked at her searchingly for a long moment. Whether or not he found what he was scanning her face for, she could not tell, but he sat back with a little sigh and allowed himself to smile.

'Your sheet?'

'My sheet,' she agreed expressionlessly.

The smile grew. 'I hope you apologised properly,' he

murmured, reaching for her hand.

'I,' she pointed out, 'have nothing to apologise for.'

'And I have.' The low voice was grave. 'I know it.'

She was flustered. 'Raoul, I didn't mean that.'

The golden eyes lifted, considered her thoughtfully. 'You know, I believe that,' he said slowly. 'You are the most extraordinary woman. You make an inordinate fuss about trifles. But where you have a real grievance—nothing.'

Philippa said with difficulty, 'I am not sure that I have a real grievance in respect of last night.' And as his eyes narrowed she went on, 'I should have told you . . .'

'Yes, I think you should,' he agreed.

'And,' she was airy, 'last night is not going to happen again.'

His mouth twitched and he said, 'That is an undeniable philosophical truth.'

'The situation is awkward. But if we talk it through . . .' she began, only to break off with a little gasp as he lifted their entwined hands and brushed his mouth casually across her knuckles.

'I agree it is not easy.' He pulled her towards him so that the light chair overbalanced and she found herself tumbled into his arms, 'But it is not something that can be helped by talking,' Raoul said firmly, kissing her.

He was only half serious, not using his full strength against her. He covered her indignant face with light, teasing kisses while she floundered to raise herself out of his arms. And then, when she thought she was free, he tipped her neatly off her chair and down on to the mossy grass, where he joined her.

'Let me up,' said Philippa, thoroughly ruffled.

'And surrender my advantage?' Raoul queried mockingly. 'You know me better than that.'

He leaned on one elbow above her, spreading her

hair in aesthetic patterns behind her head. He seemed
completely absorbed in this task though whenever she
tried to sit up she found herself blocked by the tanned
chest and subsided again. When he had fanned out the
soft dark hair to his satisfaction he began, with the most
complete coolness, to unbutton the frail blouse.

Instantly, Philippa froze.

'Stop,' she began, almost under her breath and, when
he took no notice, wailed, 'It's not fair!'

'Quite,' agreed Raoul in amusement. '*I,*' he added in
odiously virtuous tones, 'took most of my clothes off
hours ago.'

He had indeed. He was wearing only brief dark
swimming trunks and Philippa was confronted with the
naked expanse of tanned bone and muscle which made
her catch her breath on a flicker of apprehension.

'This,' he pursued, drawing the material apart so that
his mouth could drift down the valley between her
breasts to the waistband of her skirt, 'wastes time.'

But in spite of that teasing complaint he was in no
hurry. Beginning to tremble as the slow ravishment of
her senses started, Philippa realised indignantly that this
morning he was determined to make her want him with
a hunger which she would be unable to disguise or
deny. Tantalisingly, he touched his lips to one lifting
nipple and laughed as she quivered uncontrollably.

It was as different as possible from last night. There
was no hint of force; no compulsion. He was prepared,
it seemed, to take infinite pains to bring about her
subjection, but he would not, today, do anything
against her expressed will.

The blouse was pushed back, away from her body,
bunching under her arms. Philippa shifted her shoulders
uncomfortably at the constriction.

'Take it off,' Raoul said huskily.

She stared at him, green eyes wide and bemused,

cheeks flushed. He dusted a kiss over her exposed collar bone.

'Please?' he urged.

She felt swamped, stifled, choked with feeling and the fear that all his careful tactics had not succeeded in banishing.

'I—can't,' she said, unable to look at him.

'It is quite easy,' he told her in amusement, sliding his hand under the collar and easing the blouse gently away.

Under the delicate material his hand slid warmly over her shoulder, moulding it almost with love. It would be so easy, thought Philippa miserably, to take this exquisite physical courtesy for love. He lifted her, drawing the garment away from her. She felt it fall. His touch was no less gentle than the drift of muslin against her skin. A sob of pure desire caught in her throat.

Raoul tipped her face up to him, studying her expression gravely. Her breathing quickened. She caught her lower lip between her teeth and saw his eyes flare and darken. And then he was not gentle any more.

Philippa was all sensation. It was as if a dam had burst and she was swept away in the torrent. She clung to him mindlessly, glorying now in his strength, in the heavy beat of his heart against her. She strained him against her almost frantically, murmuring his name in a feverish whisper.

'Yes, darling. Yes,' Raoul said as if she had asked him for something.

She arched against him, half sobbing and then ecstasy took her. He was in every pore of her and together they were soaring in the radiant air and she would never be earthbound again.

Afterwards they lay in the absolute silence of peace. The golden head was pillowed on her breast. Philippa touched it tentatively, tenderly. And then slept.

She was awoken by the loud ringing of a bell. Raoul burrowed his head protestingly against her for a moment and then, sighing, rose.

'Damn!' he said peacefully, getting to his feet and stretching. He smiled warmly down at her. 'Don't go away.'

He hooked a towelling wrap off the back of his lounger and shrugged himself into it, strolling towards the wooden floor at the end of the garden. He disappeared and Philippa, awake and thoroughly self-conscious, scrambled to her feet, reaching for her skirt and manhandled blouse. In spite of that last injunction she had no intention of being by the pool when he returned.

She scurried back to her dressing room bearing all the appearance of one in full flight. Once there, she hurriedly found fresh underclothes, shorts and a tee shirt and descended to the kitchen area to Henriette's protection.

'I wondered if there was a map of the area,' she said a trifle breathlessly, as Henriette looked up in mild surprise from her baking.

The housekeeper nodded. 'All such things are in the study. Monsieur Raoul is still on the telephone, I suppose? It is wicked that they cannot leave him alone even on his honeymoon.'

Philippa agreed non-committally and was escorted to a large room set with bookcases and a desk the size of a family dining table.

'This is where Monsieur works,' Henriette said, smoothing a cushion in the impressive executive chair behind the desk. 'Always he brings work with him though I say here he is supposed to rest. And the maps are on the fourth shelf, there.'

Philippa extracted a smallish map of the region

which, in spite of its size, was drawn to a generous scale.

'While Monsieur is occupied I should like to explore,' Philippa told her.

'Of course. It is pointless to wait for these business calls to finish,' Henriette agreed sympathetically. 'They say women are gossips but these businessmen talk and talk. But do not go too far and tire yourself. And also you must wear something on your head because the sun here is very hot. The English are always surprised by it.'

So Philippa, bedecked in Henriette's wide-brimmed straw hat, was loosed upon the woods and waysides of her new home.

It was very green, in spite of the months of dry weather, and Philippa soon found the reason. She was traversing innumerable little fast running streams. Their banks were luxuriant with herbs and bracken as well as several trailing plants that she did not recognise. Eventually she began to pick little sprigs of flowerets, determined to ask Raoul to name them for her, on her return.

It was close and very still but she did not feel uncomfortable in the heat. Twice she stopped and paddled her feet in a clear streamlet. The water, presumably because it was fast running, was surprisingly cool. On the last occasion she leaned back with a sigh of pleasure, her hands behind her head, suffused with a sensation of wellbeing.

It would have been perfect if Raoul had only been with her. Philippa acknowledged the fact to herself with a rueful smile. She had run away from him so hard, only to find in the end that her uttermost contentment was found in his arms.

She hugged herself, remembering the sweet heaviness of his drowsing head on her breast. What if he did not love her? He wanted her and, for the moment at least, that would have to do. She herself was not sure that what she felt for him was love: it was a melting sweetness when she thought of him, a sense of fellowship, even shared laughter. And, of course, that exquisite shared peace. Did that add up to love?

She could not tell. She had not felt like this before. She had thought herself in love with Bob Sebastian. His betrayal had hurt more than anything before or since in her life. And yet had she wanted to drown in his touch, cradle his body against her, give him with prodigal hands every last thing he asked of her, as she did with Raoul?

Philippa mused, agitating the water with her feet. She had trusted Bob Sebastian almost in spite of herself; so that, while his betrayal had hurt, it had not totally surprised her. She found that she had no doubts at all about Raoul's trustworthiness. He would not hurt her and he would do all he could to shield her from harm. Philippa smiled tenderly. Not that he had said so but she knew it in her bones.

Still smiling she rose, dried her feet, put on her shoes, and set out on the return journey. She did not, even now, know what she would say to him when she next saw him. But she knew she would go straight into his arms. And she would be welcome there.

She picked up a fallen branchlet and swept the hedges with it like a child, swinging along happily, humming aloud. Within the castle walls she even broke into an eager trot, up through the multiplicity of gates and arches until she reached the coolness of the hall.

Gerard met her, his expressive face wreathed in wrinkles.

'Ah, Madame, we were worried that you might be lost. It is good that you are back. Henriette was foolish to let you go out on such a hot day. Come into the kitchen and we will give you a tisane, some iced barley water, whatever you would like.'

But Philippa shook her head, removing the borrowed hat and spinning it on her finger.

'No, I'll go and find my husband first,' she said gaily.

Gerard became even more agitated.

'Ah, Madame, that is not possible. It is a tragedy but Monsieur has had to return to Paris. The telephone, you understand. It was imperative, he says.'

Philippa stopped twirling the straw hat. The sun, which was streaming through a high window on to a polished walnut table and its vase of acanthus, seemed suddenly to have lost its warmth.

'I see,' she said slowly.

'Business, Madame. Always business,' he told her. 'It will change now he is married, Henriette and I say to each other. But he has not yet been married long enough for it to change, I think.'

She managed a smile, though it felt stiff.

'I don't think many people change when they get married, Gerard,' she said gently. 'It is not to be expected.'

He looked oddly relieved.

'Then Madame will come to the kitchen for a cold drink?' he urged.

She thanked him. Henriette, plainly waiting for her, produced a huge stone jug from a capacious refrigerator as soon as they set foot in the kitchen. It was beaded with dew at the lip and was icy to the touch.

'The juice of all the fruits,' explained Henriette, pouring some into a tall glass that frosted with shock at the cold impact. 'Orange, apricot, peach, raspberry and lemon. Very refreshing.'

Philippa, sipping, gasped with shock at the cold sweetness and then agreed with the housekeeper. Henriette beamed at her and offered a glass to Gerard who shook his head and darted out as though glad to escape. Henriette shrugged, pouring some for herself and subsiding on to a pine chair opposite Philippa.

'It is too hot to stand,' she remarked. 'There is always a jug of this in the fridge, whenever you feel thirsty, Madame. And when would you like dinner?'

Philippa made a helpless gesture. 'Whenever Monsieur Raoul returns, I suppose.'

Henriette looked at her curiously. 'But did not Gerard explain? Monsieur has gone to Paris. Mademoiselle Sebastian called and he went at once in his own plane. He will return as soon as possible, doubtless, but he said that he will definitely be away tonight.'

'Ah,' said Philippa in a hollow voice. So much for going straight into his arms! What a fool she had been. He had accomplished what he had set out to achieve, which was her willing—her more than willing— surrender, and then he had gone about his business again. No doubt he had now put her completely out of his mind. She could have afforded him no more than a little passing entertainment. Except of course that he must have been amused by the speed of her abject compliance after all her brave words.

Humiliation swept through Philippa like a dry and bitter wind. She lifted her head proudly and gave Henriette a slightly blind smile.

'At least that makes the timing of dinner easy,' she said with composure.

He stayed away three days in the end. He telephoned every morning but she told Henriette to say that she was out for a walk on each occasion. The fat housekeeper raised her eyebrows but did not protest at the required lie. And, as Philippa went out immediately afterwards and stayed out all day, it was not a complete untruth.

She had been out exploring the countryside too on

the day he returned. Toiling back up the slope from the river she saw in the distance the dust swirling behind a powerful car. And when she reached the château the Mercedes was there and a pile of pigskin luggage on the doorstep.

Philippa stepped past it cautiously and came face to face with her husband.

'At last!' Raoul exclaimed and, before she could guess his intention, had swung her up high off the ground and kissed her soundly.

He restored her to her feet, straightened her straw hat, and put her cotton blouse straight. Then he stepped back and surveyed her.

'You,' he told her in amusement, 'are going to get freckles on that lovely skin if you're not careful. It must be all this nature walking.'

Philippa bristled. That casual greeting, with its complete refusal to contemplate that she might have been hurt by his absence, had cut her to the heart. She had not expected anything else, she told herself. Ah, she added secretly, but she had hoped. Hoped that she might be wrong, that what had happened in Paris was a real crisis, that he would come back to her loving and regretful. A hearty embrace and an announcement that she was getting freckled rapidly disposed of those dreams.

'I'm sorry if you don't like freckles,' she said dulcetly, hiding her hurt. 'They're part of the package I'm afraid. I've had them since I was a child.'

Raoul patted her cheek as if he were an uncle, she thought in annoyance.

'They are delectable. Do not be concerned about them.'

'I,' she said with point, 'am not.' She looked at the suitcases and arched her fine brows. 'Have you brought friends to stay?'

At that he frowned quickly.

'Yes, you'd like that, wouldn't you?'

Philippa allowed her eyes to widen guilelessly. 'Oh, are they *my* friends? What a lovely surprise!'

'No, they are not,' Raoul snapped. 'They're your cousin Rupert's and I've agreed to give houseroom to his luggage, nothing more. He will be looking for accommodation of his own in Bordeaux. In the meantime these stay here.'

'While Rupert camps in a field?' asked Philippa sweetly. 'Really Raoul, you take your dislike of my cousin to ridiculous lengths.'

His brows closed together sharply.

'Gerard has taken Rupert into Bordeaux. I brought him back with me from Paris,' he told her harshly. 'He will be working for our factory in Bordeaux and that is where he is now, looking for a room of some kind.'

'Oh.' The hostility went out of her, almost visibly. 'Would he not wait and see me?' she asked with unconscious wistfulness.

Raoul's golden eyes narrowed. 'No doubt he would have done had I permitted it. But to tell you the truth, my dear, I had had enough of your precious cousin Rupert by the time we arrived.'

'I see,' she said in a colourless voice. 'Of course.' She straightened, aware that her shoulders were drooping in telltale fashion. 'And now you are here, I suppose you will want to refresh yourself,' she said politely. 'Have you spoken to Henriette?'

He stared at her for an unblinking moment. Then he swore under his breath.

'For God's sake Philippa, you're not my hostess.'

She flushed. He was telling her that this was his, not her, home and they had agreed that they would make no inroads into each other's possessions.

'No, of course,' she said stiltedly. 'I just wondered—

you see, Henriette likes to know when to serve dinner and I had said nine o'clock tonight. But perhaps, if you are hungry, you would like it earlier?'

Raoul's smile was a little crooked. 'I'm hungry all right. I'll show you how much if you come upstairs with me now. And I don't care if Henriette doesn't serve dinner till midnight.'

And he swept her off her feet again and ran lightly, laughing, up the wooden staircase and into their corner bedroom. He kicked the door shut with a force that sent an echo ringing round the house.

CHAPTER EIGHT

HE must, Philippa thought afterwards, have expected an easy victory. Indeed, he probably thought the battle was already lost and won. But she had been left alone for three days and she had had time, not only to castigate herself for her lack of willpower, but to rebuild her defences.

She did not waste her breath in verbal protests but struggled against him with every scrap of force at her command. She could not win, of course, against his superior strength. But she made him pause.

'Philippa,' he said with great patience, 'don't be tiresome.'

She set her teeth and would not answer or respond to him.

Raoul gave a little angry laugh. 'Are you sulking because I sent your cousin Rupert away? You should be grateful that I didn't murder him.'

Philippa wrenched her shoulders out of his grasp and retreated to the chaise longue under the window.

'What do you mean?'

'You don't know?' Raoul mocked. 'Now that's strange because Rupert assured me that he had been doing it all with your knowledge. With your co-operation, even.'

'I don't understand.'

'No, of course you don't.' Raoul's tone was dangerously sweet. 'It was all Rupert's own idea, I'm sure.'

'What was?'

'Your cousin Rupert,' he told her coldly, 'has had one last attempt at scuppering the merger. He took the

March sales figures and what I imagine were your personal projections on the basis of them, and gave them to the newspapers. It was in two of the English Sunday papers.'

Philippa stared. 'March? But they were the absolute worst. The projections I did then showed Vivian going bust in six months.'

'Precisely,' her husband agreed. 'April and May were better but Rupert obviously did not want to confuse the journalists by telling them that. As a result, I may say, I have had a hell of a time with the French papers and the banks. I have been backwards and forwards from Paris to London. I have given press conferences until I was making speeches in my sleep. I was not,' he showed his teeth in a ferocious smile, 'about to ask your cousin Rupert to spoil any more of my honeymoon. And now,' Raoul's voice roughened unmistakeably, 'come here.'

Philippa shook her head. She did not think she could speak. He had not mentioned Sally Sebastian or why he had gone to Paris in the first place. It could not have been to deal with Rupert's activities. Her uncle would have been the first person to find out, as director of Vivian Glass, and he had not made any attempt to contact Raoul at the château. So Raoul, having gone to Paris for his own private reasons, must have seen or heard of the stuff in the English papers there. And he had the effrontery to say that Rupert had ruined the honeymoon.

'You,' he told her, 'are enough to drive a man to insanity.'

Two strides brought him to her side. He picked her up without ceremony and tossed her on to the bed. Philippa struggled, her eyes over-bright, her hair swinging wildly, but he was not to be gainsaid. A gleam came into his eye as if he was actually enjoying her resistance. Philippa was enraged.

She shook the hair out of her eyes and glared up at him.

'Leave me alone,' she said between her teeth.

His eyebrows flew up.

'Are you declaring war again because I packed Rupert off to Bordeaux?' Raoul demanded incredulously. 'Don't be a fool.'

'On the contrary, I have come to my senses,' she told him, too angry to choose her words with care. 'I was a fool when I let you make love to me . . .'

He gave a soft, cruel laugh. 'It was rather more than *letting* me make love to you, as I recall, my sweet.'

She flinched, whitening. It was true. Raoul was too experienced not to have known that she had melted at his touch. She felt the ice of his contempt and turned her face away from the piercing, scornful inspection he was subjecting her to.

'Oh no,' went on the quiet, implacable voice. 'Don't turn away from me.' She was forced to face him by a sudden forceful movement of the powerful hands that held her. 'Look me in the face if you're going to lie.'

'Lie?' she said proudly.

'Yes, *lie*, damn you. I'm not a fool. I know that—last time—you wanted me as much as I wanted you. Look me in the face and deny it, if you can.'

Her lashes flickered. 'I can't,' she said sadly.

Raoul's eyes warmed. 'Well then . . .'

'But don't you see, I didn't *want* to want you?' Philippa cried. 'I don't know you. What I know I don't understand. You bully me, and tease me and abandon me——'

'But you want me,' he reminded her quietly.

And kissed her with a suffocating force that meant she could say no more.

Philippa fought strenuously but it was no use. Raoul was angry and did nothing to disguise it. In their unequal battle he gave no quarter and in her frantic attempts to escape Philippa hurt herself countless times.

In the end, of course, she ceased to struggle and her body took over, dissolving in the delight of his every movement until she cried out at the exquisite sensation.

Afterwards he did not lower his head to her breast and sleep but swung himself off the bed and began dressing with brisk movements. Philippa lay staring at him, dazed. She was breathing hard. Raoul did not look at her. She felt beaten, defeated, utterly humiliated. She turned her cheek into the pillow, willing herself not to sob out loud as the tears squeezed themselves under her eyelids.

Raoul paid her no attention. He went to the window and said with his back to her, 'I need some fresh air. I've been cooped up in cities too long. I think I'll take a horse out for an hour. Do you want to come?'

Her throat felt like sandpaper. She swallowed a couple of times before answering in a thread of a voice.

'No, thank you.'

His voice was perfectly indifferent. 'As you please. I'll see you at dinner then. Nine o'clock, I think you said?'

She agreed dully and he left, striding out of the room with impatient steps, as if he could not wait to escape. Philippa rolled over, buried her face in her hands, and for the first time since her parents died gave way to a storm of weeping.

At dinner Raoul was polite but remote. He did not mention their earlier encounter, though he told her something more of Rupert's activities. David Vivian he said was shattered by his son's disloyalty which was why he had decided to transfer Rupert to France at once. Raoul himself would have to be more in evidence at the factories and meetings, he thought, as a result of the renewed speculation. Confidence had been lost and would only be restored by a firm hand being seen at the helm.

'Does that mean you will have to go back to Paris?' Philippa asked, not knowing if she was relieved or disappointed.

He darted her an unsmiling look.

'Would you mind?'

'No, of course not. You have to do whatever is necessary for the company, I realise that. I just thought that—if we were not keeping up this fiction of a honeymoon——' she explained with difficulty, 'I might go back to London.'

He smote his fist down on the table so that the glasses jumped at the impact.

'You will stay here if I have to lock you in your room.' He drew a deep breath and calmed himself with a visible effort. 'We said a month, and that's what we shall take. I can visit the factories easily enough from here if I pilot myself. Your—er—holiday shall not be interrupted.'

And with that she had to be content.

He came and went unpredictably, never telling Philippa where he was going or when he would return. She was too proud to complain, especially as it was plain that Henriette and Gerard knew all about his movements. When they met she tried to be civil to him like, he once said in a fury, a polite schoolgirl.

Left on her own all day she explored the countryside on foot, armed with a map and a small guide to the local trees and plants. Sometimes she would bring home specimens and mount them. She even tried her hand at painting them in watercolours that Gerard brought her from Bordeaux. In her determination not to sink into self-pity she became absorbed in this new hobby.

So absorbed was she that, on occasions, she would forget that Raoul was the enemy and enter into quite friendly conversations about local sights or plants. But the friendliness dissolved all too soon after dark.

Sometimes he left her to sleep alone. But when he did she lay awake and tense, listening for sounds in his room that might indicate that he was about to open the connecting doors and rip her peace of mind from her again.

He never spoke, never answered her pleas or her protests. He was not violent, either, but he was determined, and every time that Philippa acquiesced in the glorious use the powerful golden body made of hers, she knew that another fragment of her self respect had been chipped away. He had told her, ages ago before they were married, that he wanted to destroy her cool self-possession and he had succeeded. She had found ecstasy in his arms only to have to pay the price of bitter regret afterwards.

She grew thinner. She was spending too much time in the open air to grow pale but her face took on a nervous, pointed look and her green eyes began to look haunted. Henriette and Gerard noticed and were unobtrusively concerned. Raoul never mentioned it, seeming not to see the change in her.

And Philippa herself, refusing to be broken by the force of this unwelcome emotion, walked and drew and painted as if her life depended on it.

Eventually, after dinner one evening, her control broke. It was a hot night and the windows on to the terrace had been left open. After their meal, at which Philippa had been able to do no more than nibble, they took their wine out on to the terrace where a faint breeze stirred the vine. She leant her elbows on the balustrade looking out over the drowsing fields in the twilight. Raoul came up beside her and touched her arm gently. She jumped and swung round, swift as a snake.

'*Don't!*' she cried on an involuntary breath.

He said quietly, 'Philippa, you can't go on like this. You'll make yourself ill.'

She drew back. 'I'm sorry. I didn't mean to screech. You startled me.'

Raoul sighed. 'That's exactly my point. You're as tense as a cat. Why?'

In the darkness her smile was twisted. 'You could say that I'm not used to being married, I suppose.'

Raoul was silent for a moment. Then he said gravely, 'Is it really that bad?'

She turned away. 'Oh, I'll get used to it in time, I expect,' she said in a brittle voice. 'But it's all so new— living with other people, servants, being in a strange place, having to follow a timetable, not having my own work to do . . .'

'And having to let me make love to you,' Raoul supplied ironically.

'Y-yes.'

'Philippa——' he paused, apparently at a loss. 'What happened? What went wrong? I thought . . .'

'That you had won,' she finished for him. 'Well, you had. You have.'

'Don't say that,' Raoul told her fiercely. 'It's not a battle. The hostility, the hate is all on your side. I told you, it doesn't have to be like that. But you look at me sometimes as if you expect me to hurt you.'

She made no answer. She could not.

'Philippa, look at me.' He turned her towards him with unaccustomed gentleness. 'Are you afraid of me?'

She swallowed. 'Yes,' she admitted in a small shamed voice.

Raoul was very still. 'Why?' he said at last. 'What has happened to you that makes you like this? One could almost imagine you had been raped . . .'

Philippa gave a harsh laugh. He stopped.

'It can't be true,' he said slowly. 'I'll swear I was the first. I didn't believe it, it seemed so utterly unlikely. But I *know* it was so. Wasn't it?'

'Oh yes,' she acknowledged in a high, strained voice, 'I was a virgin. Top marks for observation.'

Raoul swore under his breath and shook her slightly but she went on, reckless of angering him.

'Which is odd, really, when you think of the way I seem to attract violence. No, as you point out, I hadn't been raped before we married. Not quite.'

His hands tightened like a steel brace until she felt her bones would snap.

'Who——' he began but she could not stop now that her control had gone, her voice soaring bitterly.

'And as for since—Well what do you call what you have been doing to me if it isn't rape?'

She stopped, aware of a queer feeling of pain and despair. She had burnt her boats now, she thought in panic. He would never forgive her now.

Raoul said in a deadly voice, 'You don't mean that.'

Philippa bent her head, clasping her hands round her. The glass in her right hand was shaking so much that some of the wine slopped out on to her bare toes.

He said furiously, 'You're a child. A stupid, spoilt, neurotic child. Why——? Oh, go to the devil your own way. I've had enough of your whole damned family.'

And he left her on the darkening terrace and went through the dining room, slamming the door behind him so that the candles still burning on the table flared and danced. Philippa did not see him again for two days.

She did, however, see the result of his handiwork. A long letter from her uncle arrived, enclosing a number of press cuttings whose import made her shudder. Uncle David was full of praise for Raoul. He could not have been more helpful. It was obvious that he was impatient to get back to Philippa of course, but he had nevertheless bent all his energies to rescuing them from the mess Rupert had got them into.

Aunt Margaret also wrote, a more subdued letter. She did not mention Raoul except to say that he had been furious about the newspapers. There was also a slight hint that Raoul had not been in London alone which Philippa took to mean that Sally Sebastian had accompanied him. And indeed, there in one of the magazines that her aunt had sent her, admittedly of a date which preceded the wedding by a couple of weeks, was a photograph of Raoul entering a restaurant with the charming Miss Sebastian and another man. Philippa tried hard to pretend that she did not care.

When Raoul himself eventually appeared again at the dinner table his whole manner made it plain that he, for his part, was completely indifferent. He talked fluently and amusingly but he had retired behind a film of ice. Philippa had the feeling that he would have been equally pleasant to a stranger, even one he disliked.

Their days fell into a pattern. Raoul rose early, swam and was generally breakfasted and gone by the time Philippa came downstairs. She would then swim and take one of her prolonged walks about the countryside. They would meet over cocktails in the evening and make polite, dead conversation. The only subject on which they approached each other without reserve was the manufacture and marketing of glass.

One day Philippa said wistfully, as Raoul was describing a process for smoking multicoloured glass, 'Oh, I wish I could see it.'

He shot her a sharp look but said with unshadowed cordiality, 'You're welcome if you would like to come and see it done. You could join me tomorrow.'

Philippa was shocked at the surge of pleasure that this olive branch gave her. She suppressed it, looking doubtful.

'I wouldn't want to be in the way.'

'You wouldn't be. Not as long as you stood quietly and watched, you know that. It would be a good education for you to see a French factory in operation, since you are now a director of a French company,' Raoul told her teasingly.

More than anything she wanted to go with him. If only he would say that he wanted her company, urge her to come in some way. But he did not.

'Where are you going tomorrow? Which factory?' asked Philippa, playing for time.

'Delice. Just outside Bordeaux.'

She gave up the attempt to fight herself.

'I'd love to come,' she told him, with a shy smile.

He nodded coolly, not seeming to notice that this was an olive branch in its turn. Or perhaps he had lost interest in olive branches from her, thought Philippa. Her smile faded.

He was as remote as ever the next morning, putting her into the Mercedes with formal courtesy. As they drove off she looked about her with pleasure.

'It is so beautiful here.'

For the moment his face softened. 'Yes, you've acclimatised better than I had hoped. You really like it, don't you?'

'How could anyone not?' she said, turning in her seat to watch the château on its little pinnacle recede behind them.

The factory, by contrast, was in the most modern of air conditioned buildings. Philippa stepped gratefully into the frigid atmosphere, shaking the damp hair away from the back of her neck with a little movement of pure pleasure. She found Raoul's eyes on her, unfathomable and yellow as a cat's. She raised her eyebrows at him but there was no time for conversation because the factory manager was upon them. They were shown round with considerable ceremony which Philippa suggested was primarily for her benefit. Raoul seemed to get on well with everyone and though they treated his opinions with respect there was nothing deferential in their manner.

Philippa was slightly surprised. She would have expected him to be as dictatorial at work as he had proved at home. This democratic camaraderie with his employees disconcerted her. Perhaps it was only for her that Raoul reserved that imperious manner? It was reasonable enough: he respected his employees and despised her.

She began to hang back slightly, talking with the production manager. He was a middle-aged Bordelais, brown as a nut and with an accent as strong as his tan. It took all her concentration and years of fluency in the language for Philippa to make out what he was saying. He, for his part, was charmed that the patron's new wife could ask sensible questions and was all set to allow her to try parts of the process herself. Raoul, however, stopped him, 'We must not interrupt the output, darling,' he told her, his face like thunder.

'No, of course not.' Philippa was bewildered but did her best to hide it. She turned to the production manager to thank him and found that he was looking distinctly wary. He made placatory noises to Raoul but could not disguise his relief when they left without further conversation.

In the car Raoul rounded on her.

'Why the hell did you lie about speaking French?'

She flushed. She recalled that she had decided to tell him of her linguistic ability on the day of their wedding. But events since then had put it out of her head. And the Longines' English was so good she had not used it.

'I forgot,' she said lamely.

He started the motor with a savage flick of the wrist.

'Forgot!' he mocked. 'Like you forgot to tell me that your cousin Rupert was going to shop the company? Like you forgot to tell me you were a virgin? God, you must hate me.'

'No!' Philippa half turned to him, protesting passionately at his mistake.

She must have distracted him momentarily from his concentration on the road. At least, he did not seem to notice the approach of a small van, labouring up the incline in the middle of the road.

'Look out!' she gasped.

Raoul swore and hauled the wheel round, sending the big car scraping along the hedge to avoid the oncoming van. The steering wheel span in his hands as the tyres hit baked earth and skidded. The car rocked, tilted, rocked again and then fell with a scream of agonised machinery on to its side into the hedge.

Philippa jerked forward, back and sideways against the door. She heard, as from a great distance, her name called hoarsely. Then her head met the glass of the side window with a smart crack and she knew no more.

CHAPTER NINE

THERE were bees buzzing and the light hurt her eyes. She turned her head fretfully on a pillow as hard as a board. Raoul was angry with her and had made her sleep on timber as a punishment. She moaned.

'Hush. Oh, my darling, hush,' said a voice she knew could not be Raoul's.

She winced, turning her head away from the voice, the light, from all the things that she dimly realised she was not ready to deal with.

Another voice said, 'Monsieur, you must realise she is not conscious. She does not know you. Do not distress yourself.'

And then it went black again and she remembered no more.

They told her afterwards that the Comte had sat by her bedside for two whole days. But as she began to recover it seemed that his presence had made her restive. So they had asked him to leave. But he was most anxious about the health of his young wife, most attentive. He telephoned every night. And if she wanted to see him, no doubt Dr Brouilly would consider it.

At that Philippa had shaken her head decisively. She was not, she knew, strong enough for a confrontation with Raoul yet; not when she recalled how angry he had been before the car crashed. Seeing her pinched face and frightened eyes, the nurses did not try to persuade her otherwise.

Eventually, of course, she was discharged, though with a warning to take things easily for a while. Head injuries, they intimated, could be unpredictable.

She was driven back to the château by Gerard, unwontedly subdued. Monsieur Raoul, he explained, had had to go back to work. But Henriette would take good care of Madame until he returned.

Philippa thanked him absently. In the hospital she had had plenty of time to think about the explosive tension that existed between Raoul and herself. In the past she had ascribed it to her own wariness, her unfortunate brush with Bob Sebastian, her parents disastrous marriage, her natural taste for the solitary life. And of course it was complicated by the intense attraction that he exerted. Now, however, she knew it was more than that. She was in love with him. She wanted to be welcome in his life, she wanted to be his true love; she wanted him to come home to her and only to her. She wanted the right to enquire into his affairs and lend her aid if it was needed. She wanted to be allowed to love him.

It was, she also realised, quite hopeless. Though Raoul would be ready enough to take her to bed, if she indicated that was what she wanted, he had never shown any sign of wanting anything else. Indeed, she had every reason to believe that he had avoided involvement all his life and would continue to do so. If she poured out her unwanted love, the best that she could achieve would be that he would accept it. The worst, and she felt sick as she imagined it, would be his bewildered embarrassment. She knew she could not bear that.

So, when he telephoned meticulously every night to enquire after her health, she answered him cheerfully, amusingly, giving no hint of her feelings.

'You'd think I was a piece of old and precious glass,' she told him lightly on one such occasion. 'If I so much as turn my ankle either Gerard or Henriette leaps forward to catch me. They seem to think I'll shatter at any moment.'

Raoul laughed but said too, 'You must not underestimate the shock. And you did not look—well— before the accident. They are right to take care.'

'I'm better now,' she protested. 'And I'm getting bored. I think I shall go back to London.'

He gave a low chuckle at that. 'I assure you, you won't. I have taken the precaution of removing your passport,' he informed her. And, while she was speechless with outrage, wished her a cool goodnight and rang off.

Philippa might be helplessly in love with him but she was not so besotted that she did not resent this piece of high handedness. It would, she thought wistfully, have been different if he had loved her. But she had no doubt that he did not. He made no attempt during his dutiful telephone calls to disguise his indifference. He never asked how she spent her day, whether she was happy; or if she was missing him. Very well, determined Philippa, she would *not* miss him.

And then, one day, though Henriette tried to prevent her from seeing it, came the inevitable gossip column. Philippa was not new to French newspapers but she could not judge how well informed the columnist was likely to be. It all sounded only too plausible to her, though.

'Comte Raoul de Martin, who only eight weeks ago surrendered his long-defended bachelor status,' [said the article] 'was seen at the opera last night with former girlfriend, Janssisse executive, Sally Sebastian. The dashing Comte, who looked tired and preoccupied, had nothing to say to our reporter. Lively Mademoiselle Sebastian said they were still friends and business contacts. The missing Comtesse is said to be recovering in one of her husband's many rural retreats after a small accident. All her friends must wish her a speedy return to her health.'

It was a nasty thing. Philippa let the paper fall from her hands, feeling the words crawl over her skin like prickly heat. She gave a little shudder of disgust. She looked up to find Gerard regarding her with passionate sympathy.

'These journalists!' he snorted, finding her eyes upon him. 'They will say anything. It is jealousy, for the most part. They are silly old men who no woman would go out with and they envy Monsieur . . .' He broke off, realising that his intended comfort might be less than consoling.

Philippa gave him a determined smile.

'Monsieur has certainly given them plenty to write about,' she agreed.

'That was in the past,' Gerard pointed out swiftly, 'Before his marriage. He will not, now, . . .' He made an expansive gesture to indicate the enormity of behaviour from which Raoul would now refrain.

'It seems, however, that he has,' Philippa pointed out gently.

Gerard was upset. It must surely be an error, an exaggeration. Monsieur would take steps to stop such things being printed.

'I'm sure he will,' Philippa concurred with an irony which Gerard missed.

There would be a retraction, he promised, encouraging himself more than her. He brightened as he described the grovelling terms in which Raoul would demand the paper's apology be couched. Philippa listened and responded suitably but inside she felt numb.

It could not be more obvious that Raoul simply did

not care at all, she thought. He must be keeping her a virtual prisoner here out of a misplaced sense of duty. She knew he had blamed himself for the accident. Now he must be determined that she regain her full strength before he released himself from the obligation to care for her.

So she would assure him that she had regained that strength. And then she would leave the château, return to London and take up her old life as if nothing had happened. And eventually, as they had always intended, they would get a quiet divorce and she would be free of him.

Except, thought Philippa desolately, she would never be free. She looked down at the paper in her hands. They had printed old photographs of Raoul and Sally to go with the story. Raoul looked handsome as the devil, his eyes alight with that laughter that turned her bones to water. And Sally, caught in profile at some party, looked a match for him: relaxed, sophisticated, wearing the diamonds in her ears and the untidiest of casual coiffures with the nonchalance of a true jet setter. They were two of a kind.

Philippa stood up decisively. It was intolerable to be languishing here in the château, living from telephone call to telephone call, eating her heart out for one word that might hint that he cared for her. He did not. He had never pretended that he did. And if she had taken the ultimate stupid step and fallen in love with him, then it was up to her to get out fast—before Raoul found her out to his and her own embarrassment. She must go and as soon as possible.

As a first step she had Gerard drive her to the doctor's consulting rooms for a thorough examination. Gerard was worried but she managed to convince him that it was no more than a routine visit after her accident.

The doctor looked her over impassively, did a number of tests on her sight and hearing, and then seated himself behind his desk.

'There seems to be no permanent damage from your injuries,' he told her cautiously.

Philippa expelled a little breath of relief. 'I thought there was not. But I had to be sure, for my husband's sake.'

She blushed faintly. It always gave her a slight shock to refer to Raoul in that way. He still seemed so completely free; it felt like an encroachment into his private space to lay claim to him in that telling little word. The doctor considered the blush thoughtfully.

'Of course, your husband was driving, was he not? It is always the worst part: to bear the responsibility for damaging someone we love.'

Philippa flinched but managed a faint smile in response.

'In this case, fortunately, your husband has been spared that. And as the driver of the other vehicle was unhurt, all ends well. But you, Madame, I do not think that you are well and it has nothing to do with a few cuts and bruises from the accident.'

He paused hopefully, but Philippa still said nothing.

He sighed, 'Madame de Martin, I do not know your husband. But by reputation he is a very strong personality. You are alone, in a strange country, newly married. You may well feel off balance.' His voice gentled. 'It would not be disloyal of you to feel that, or to tell your doctor if you did.'

Philippa raised her head. 'All I am asking for is a clean bill of health so that I can go back to work,' she told him coolly.

He shrugged helplessly. 'If that is your wish. But—is there no one of your own family in France, Madame, to whom you could talk perhaps?'

She smiled. 'My cousin has been here a few weeks.'

'Well, see him,' he urged. 'It is surprising what a comfort a familiar face can be.'

She thanked him and left, her mouth quirking in private amusement. It would be fun to see Rupert but he would not be flattered to know that her doctor had recommended that she use him like a sticking-plaster, she thought.

And then, as she turned into the gates she saw the Mercedes. Her pulses gave a great leap and then steadied. She got out of the car and met Raoul. Carefully she veiled the transparent delight in her eyes.

'How nice to see you. Are you *en route* or will you be staying?'

Raoul's eyes narrowed. 'Do you care at all?' he asked softly.

She gave a slight shrug. 'It would be convenient for Henriette to know.'

His expression revealed nothing as he said smoothly, 'Of course. Well, for Henriette's sake then I have to tell you that this is a flying visit only.'

Philippa murmured conventional regret to which he listened with a distinctly cynical smile. He motioned her to sit down.

'They tell me you have been to the doctor,' Raoul said abruptly. 'Why?'

She stared at him. 'F-for a check up,' she stammered, disconcerted by his tone.

He looked at her oddly.

'Why?' he said again. 'You have pain, perhaps? The headaches they warned of?'

She shook her head. 'No.'

Raoul reached out a hand and put it firmly under her chin, forcing her to look at him. The yellow eyes were unfathomable, remote as the desert.

'You will not lie to me, if you please. Are you pregnant?'

The colour washed up into her cheeks in a great flood at the cool question. She glared at him indignantly, trying to hide her confusion.

'That's a very personal question.'

Raoul's smile did not reach his eyes.

'Quite a permissible one from a husband, I would have thought. Are you?'

She shook her head. 'I—I don't think so. I—It never occurred to me.'

He gave a sharp sigh, dropping her chin and turning away from her swiftly.

'You're such a child, sometimes. You make me despair. Well, now you have thought of it, could you be?'

Philippa flushed again but bent her mind to calculation obediently. At length she said baldly, 'No.'

He let out a long breath. 'Well, at least I haven't done that to you,' he said almost to himself. 'So why did you visit the doctor?'

Philippa gave him a look of dislike. 'For a check up, I told you. I want to go back to work.'

'Work?' The beautiful dark eyebrows rose lazily.

'My job,' she reminded him sweetly. 'From which I am still on holiday thanks to your tactics.'

He gave a grin suddenly and dived a hand inside the breast pocket of his jacket. He brought out the dark blue British passport that he had purloined.

'You mean when I requisitioned this? But what else was I to do? I did not want you running off back to London when my back was turned.'

Philippa resisted the temptation to snatch at it. From his tantalising expression he had every hope that she would do just that. And then no doubt he would whip it high out of her reach. He had more than a touch of devilment in his smile at the moment.

She let her cool green gaze just flicker an

acknowledgment at the passport and sat back on her chair, crossing one slim leg over the other. She permitted herself a slow smile.

'I shall tell them it has been stolen and apply for another,' she told him charmingly.

'Yes, you'd do that, wouldn't you?' His voice was amused, rueful, full of reluctant respect. He tossed the small book across the table at her. 'There you are then. Since you are prepared to bring the full force of the British Passport Office into the field against me, I can see that I have lost the battle.'

Philippa smiled as she was clearly intended to do. She picked up the passport slowly. Was this a way of telling her that he wanted her to leave the château? She smoothed the leaves of the booklet with fingers that shook.

'I'll go back to London next week,' she told him. 'If that's all right?' she added, suddenly wondering if he wanted her gone urgently; if he wanted to bring Sally to this house now. The thought cut like a knife. She turned her head away from him so he should not read the truth in her expression.

Raoul said slowly, 'Did the doctor agree?'

She did not answer.

'I see. So he did not.'

'I didn't tell him that I wanted to go back to London,' she explained. 'I didn't know whether it might embarrass you.'

'That was thoughtful.' She did not know whether he was being ironic. 'Thank you. But he obviously said something that you don't want to tell me. What was it?'

A little gust of fury shook her. If he did not love her what right did he have to probe like this?

'If you must know, he told me I needed to see Rupert,' she snapped. *That*, she thought, ought to stop any more of his damned unanswerable questions.

'*What?*' Raoul sounded as if he did not believe his ears. He had clearly expected something very different.

She shrugged. 'That's what he said.'

'And I wonder,' said Raoul between his teeth, 'what *you* had said to produce such a convenient prescription.'

The schoolboy mischief was all gone now. He looked what he was, a tough, capable and cruelly attractive man in a raging temper. It was extraordinary, thought Philippa, slightly alarmed, the way he reacted whenever Rupert's name was mentioned. You would have thought Rupert was some deep and personal enemy. Whereas, in fact, Rupert had only slightly impeded the planned merger. And surely Raoul must be used to such temporary commercial setbacks. Surely he could not react so violently to everybody who ever crossed him.

You crossed him, she reminded herself. Her thoughts went flying back to that devastating evening in Paris. He had been in a temper then. So perhaps that was the answer. He was no longer fierce with her because he had beaten her. Remembering just how he had brought about her submission, Philippa began to tremble inwardly with long sweet shudders that made her dread his detection.

She said at random, 'The doctor seemed to think I needed someone of my own in France.'

Raoul began to smile; it was the clever, cynical smile she dreaded. It said that he knew all her most intimate thoughts, every last secret place of her body, and how they all responded to him.

'A husband does not qualify?' he asked with dangerous quietness.

She knew what would happen next. The tone more than the words made it plain to her shrinking senses. He would reach for her, take her against him, and all her careful defences would not be enough to withhold from him the knowledge that she was his to do with what he wanted for as long as he wanted. Oh God, she loved him and if he touched her now there would be no way she could hide it from him.

She said, in real panic and not in answer to his spoken question, *'No!'*

He hesitated, his mouth twisting. Slowly the danger seemed to seep out of him. He lifted one shoulder negligently, as if the whole matter were not worth bothering further about.

'Then you had better invite him, hadn't you?' The brilliant eyes were hooded, the voice quite without emotion. 'Since you have gone to such lengths to get his presence—er—recommended on medical advice. Telephone him and ask him for the weekend.'

She stared uncomprehending. 'Y-you mean ask Rupert here?' She blinked. 'Will you be here?'

At that his anger blazed into life again, though she did not know what she had said to rekindle it.

'Yes, I damned well will. And so will my guests. Unless,' with ferocious mockery, 'the good doctor recomended you to see your cousin Rupert alone?'

Philippa shook her head, quite bewildered.

'Good. Then I hope that I and my friends will not intrude. I will tell Henriette which rooms to prepare.' He bent and kissed her, a brief hard assault on her mouth, more of a challenge than an embrace. 'I must go. I will see you on Friday. And Rupert, of course.'

CHAPTER TEN

HENRIETTE's pleasure at having a houseful of guests for the weekend was deep and uncomplicated.

'It will be just like the old days,' she told Philippa with an approving look. 'When the Comtesse was alive we entertained a lot. Monsieur Raoul would say she was frivolous but he would come too. He was different in those days, very light hearted, very popular . . .'

'He seems popular enough now,' observed Philippa drily. She thought of Sally Sebastian and felt again that queer ache that always struck her when she imagined Raoul in company with another woman.

She shook herself mentally. It was ridiculous. He would always be in company with other women. It was inevitable. With his charm, that dangerous attractiveness, to say nothing of his wealth and influence, it would be ridiculous to expect anything else. It was not even as if she had a right to expect anything else, not after the terms she herself had set on their marriage.

She found Henriette regarding her narrowly.

'He changed overnight when his father died,' the cook said. 'It was the shock—there were so many debts you see. You would not know it, now, but Gerard and I remember. He sold everything: the apartment in Paris, the place in Savoy, the pictures, the jewels, the cars. He would have sold the château as well but Madame became so ill and it was her home. As it was he sold off fields, woodland, piece by piece. And all the time he was working so hard.' She sighed her comfortable face saddened at the memory she had conjured up. 'The

Comtesse used to say to me sometimes, "All his youth is going Henriette." She blamed herself, you know.'

Philippa was curious. She had never stopped to consider how Raoul's wealth had been acquired. He had simply been the unwelcome millionaire come to salvage and plunder her uncle's firm. Perhaps it was that unpromising start that had given him the hard, almost cruel drive that she admired in the businessman and feared in the husband.

'Did the Comtesse never know that he was successful?' she asked. 'When did she die?'

Henriette sighed. 'She knew and she did not like it. She said he had lost his humanity.'

'What?' Philippa was astounded. It was a vivid phrase and not, she thought, one that would come naturally to the simple housekeeper.

'I heard her tell him so, oh many times.'

'But—but *why*?'

'She did not like the things he did. Or his friends. She said he treated everyone as if he were an enemy, including the women. If they flattered him, he despised them. And if they did not, he broke them.' Henriette looked at Philippa miserably. 'That's what the Comtesse used to say, you understand, Madame,' she added, misinterpreting Philippa's expression. 'And, of course, it is different since he has married. The Comtesse would have been so pleased. And now to be entertaining again . . .'

And she was off, with a long list of suggestions for the weekend's arrangements. Philippa agreed with them all, absently. She hardly heard the cheerful catalogue. She felt chilled to the bone by Henriette's revelations.

She thought of the first time they had met. Oh no, she had certainly not flattered him. He must have expected her to do so. God knows, Vivians had needed his money and they both knew it. But she had been hostile. He had disconcerted her, even frightened her a little. No she had not flattered him. She had barely been conciliating.

And so he had set out on that other path; to break her.

Philippa sank on to a sofa and dropped her head in her hands in a gesture of complete despair. But why on earth had he gone so far as to marry her? It was surely unnecessary and had caught him as much as herself in the trap. If he was so driven to dominate anyone who showed him opposition, why had he not simply sacked her from the firm, after he took it over? Or employed her somewhere where she had to dance to his tune? Why marriage? It did not make sense.

But everything else did. It all fitted too horribly. The determination to separate her from her family, even from Rupert; the refusal to let her go back to work; even his fury when he found that she could speak his language and was not therefore so helpless in his country as he had thought she was. It all came to the same sum: he wanted her in his power. Utterly and without access to anything that had been important in her life before she met him.

She shivered, pressing her knuckles against eyes that ached but were tearless. Even when he made love to her—her mouth was dry remembering it—even then, there was no love or kindness but only that demonic determination to make her respond to him. It was all an exercise in power. A highly successful exercise, she thought bitterly. His power over her was very nearly complete. And not because of his strategy but because she herself had put all the weapons in his hands by falling in love with him.

The shame of it, of falling in love with a man to whom she was no more than a piece of terrain to be conquered, began to seep through her corrosively. She tried to ignore it, to go about the business of preparing for the guests in a sensible way, but she felt as if she were wrapped in an invisible mist which kept her chilly and frightened and cut off from human contact. When Raoul telephoned, she spoke to him in cool tones which lifted Gerard's eyebrows, though it brought no obvious reaction from her husband.

But when Rupert arrived on a Friday night, elegant and just a little sheepish, Philippa felt as if she had received a blessed visitation from a Paradise from which she had been banished. In a spontaneous rush of pleasure she flung herself into the startled Rupert's arms.

'Oh, it's so good to see you,' she said, pressing her cold cheek against his.

He hugged her. 'And, you, Pipps. And you. I wasn't sure you'd have me over the threshold after the Great Disgrace.'

She laughed, turning and drawing his arm through her own.

'I don't know very much about the Great Disgrace. You'd better tell me all about it. It will make me feel part of the family again,' she teased, taking him into the château.

Gerard was waiting in the marble floored hallway, ready to take the arriving guest's suitcases to his room. He looked stiff, disapproving even. Philippa began to wonder if he did not share his wife's delight in entertaining and resented the additional work.

She withdrew her hand from Rupert's arm and said, 'You know my cousin, Rupert Vivian, don't you, Gerard? Would you take his cases to the chintz room, please?'

'Certainly, Madame,' said Gerard with chilling formality. 'If you will follow me, sir?'

He turned in a stately manner, far removed from his usual scamper and advanced along the hall with a measured tread. Rupert looked taken aback and exchanged a startled glance with his cousin. Philippa shook her head slightly, indicating bewilderment and Rupert broke into his wicked grin.

Gerard turned and found them exchanging conspiratorial looks like naughty children. His aspect became even more glacial.

'*This* way, sir.'

With his compelling eye on them there was nothing else to be done. Rupert looked at her helplessly, gave a shrug and then strolled off in Gerard's wake.

Philippa found herself not only puzzled but faintly dismayed by the odd little scene. Why Gerard should resent Rupert she could not imagine, yet plainly he did. Perhaps it was a reflection of Raoul's dislike? Raoul, after the bad publicity that her cousin had whipped up, had reason enough to dislike Rupert. But surely he would not stoop to instructing the servant to make Rupert feel uncomfortable? If he did not want him in his house he need not have asked him.

She was pondering the problem, her brows faintly creased, when Rupert found her in the rose garden. He had taken off his city suit and tie and was wearing a pair of light cord trousers and an open-necked shirt, looking infinitely cooler and more relaxed than when he had arrived.

'Phew!' he said, coming towards her and wiping mock sweat from his brow with the back of his hand. 'That's better. I always rather fancied the life of the idle rich but I don't think I could endure the aged retainer for long. Is he always like that?'

Philippa shook her head. 'No. I can't think why . . .'

He gave her a wry look.

'Can't you?' he said sinking down beside her on the iron work seat and linking his hands behind his head. 'Seemed to me he knew a black sheep when he saw one and didn't mind showing it.'

Philippa was indignant. 'He has no right to do anything of the kind and so I shall tell him.'

Rupert stretched out a hand and covered her. 'Don't bother, Pipps. You'll only add fuel to the fire. Anyway, he's right.' The bantering voice had a hint of pain in it. 'I'm only surprised you don't feel the same way. My father told me that—well——' he took his hand away and gave an embarrassed shrug, 'that you more or less had to marry de Martin to save our skin.'

She was speechless. Finding her silent, he went on quickly and in a more serious tone than she had ever heard him use, 'And I taunted you with it. I thought that, like every other woman in the world, you wanted a man with money. I'm sorry, Pipps.'

He turned his face towards the sun, as if he was basking in its rays, but there was a hint of colour on his cheekbones that showed he was not as nonchalant as he pretended. Philippa was touched, albeit slightly amused. Rupert would not find it easy to apologise.

'But I did want a man with money,' she pointed out gravely. 'A poor man would have been no use to Vivians.'

'Nor would any other rich man,' he countered swiftly. 'And you didn't want to marry him, either, did you? He's not your type.'

Philippa shrugged, looking away. She could not answer him.

'God knows why he wanted you,' Rupert said with sudden violence. 'Why couldn't he have stuck to his own kind? The jet setting ladies have been after him for years. If he wanted to marry, there was no reason to go and mess up the life of someone like you.'

She felt as if she could not bear it. In a few short sentences Rupert had brought to the surface all her own most private misgivings. For a moment the urge to confide in someone else was almost overwhelming. But then she recollected herself.

It was private not only to herself but to Raoul. She could not discuss him with anyone, not even her cousin. It felt like betrayal even to think of it.

She said gently, 'I chose to marry him, Rupert.'

He stopped, as if struck. Then, very slowly, he turned his head to look down at her, squinting slightly in the sunlight. There was a pause.

Then he said slowly, almost with horror, 'I think you've fallen in love with him.'

She flushed, a deep betraying blush that washed through her in an uncontrollable tide. But she was spared having to answer because at that moment she heard the unmistakeable crash of the heavy main doors as they swung back on their ancient hinges. There could be no doubt about the meaning of that noise. Gerard must have opened them as a piece of deliberate ceremony to indicate to all concerned that the master of the house had returned.

Philippa jumped to her feet, flustered.

'Raoul must have arrived,' she said to Rupert unnecessarily. 'I didn't expect ... That is I thought ... He is earlier than he said he would be.'

Her cousin surveyed her with a frown as she turned, with less than her accustomed composure, to the house. Before she had gone three steps, the cause of her agitation appeared at the french window. He halted for a moment, considering them, his face unreadable. Then he came at an unhurried pace down the shallow steps and through the arch of trailing roses towards them.

'Good afternoon,' he said pleasantly to Rupert.

And then, before she had any warning of his intentions, he took Philippa by the upper arms and gave her a hard kiss. For a moment his eyes lightened, plainly amused by the confusion that his action caused her. Then the steady gaze shifted to Rupert and became opaque again.

'You're early,' said Philippa, wishing she did not sound as if she were trying to excuse herself, even as she said it. 'We—I didn't hear a car.'

'No doubt you were too wrapped up in discussing old times,' Raoul agreed suavely, seating himself in the ironwork seat she had just vacated. 'Rupert too is early.' He addressed her cousin. 'I did not think you could be here before it was dark.'

Rupert flushed. 'I took the afternoon off,' he said belligerently. 'I wanted to talk to Pipps without interruptions.' It was very nearly rude.

Raoul's eyes narrowed though his voice, when he spoke, sounded more amused than anything else. 'And so, too, did I. It seems we have both wasted our time.'

Turning in bewilderment from one man to the other, Philippa realised that Raoul's whole demeanour was a challenge. There was nothing overt about it, nothing to which she or Rupert could take exception. It was all very smooth and restrained and polite. But it was there nevertheless; negligent, half amused but quite implacable. Raoul was lord of his corner of the human jungle and Rupert flouted his authority at his peril.

Philippa shivered. She did not think she had ever before felt so much in Raoul's power, so utterly a *thing*, as she did standing between them like a bone between two dogs. She moved away.

'You must both be thirsty,' she said in a cool little voice. 'The roads are so dusty in this heat. I will tell Henriette to bring tea out here as soon as possible.' And she left them confronting each other.

The rest of the day was a nightmare. It seemed as if a demon of perversity had entered into Rupert. He disagreed with Raoul's slightest remark. He was polite, of course, but he fairly bristled with hostility. Raoul treated him with amusement bordering on contempt but, for his part, let no opportunity go by to touch Philippa, making his ownership plain, she thought with pain. She did not respond by so much as a flicker of an eyelash, suffering the arm about her shoulders, the hand at the nape of her neck, as if she were not even aware she was being touched. But her nerves tautened.

And Rupert interpreted every gesture as a personal insult. Why, she could not imagine. Unless he was still suffering from a troubled conscience for his part in helping to pitchfork her into a marriage with a man who did not love her. It was all too probable that his indignation was on her account rather than his own, Philippa thought. Rupert bore all the signs of suffering from a bad attack of remorse.

She tried to persuade him that it was not necessary but without success. The antipathy between the two men was so strong that all her efforts only served to increase their hostility. Giving up hope of reconciling them, she made her excuses early in the evening, pleading the need to bath and dress before the visitors arrived.

Raoul gave her a mocking look. He knew exactly how long it took her to get ready for dinner. He also knew, therefore, that she was running away. But he did not try to detain her.

She was soaking in a lavishly scented bath when she discovered the reason for his forbearance. Without warning the door opened and Raoul strolled in casually, as if he invaded her bathroom every day of his life. Philippa sat bolt upright in a splashing surge of water that sprayed his immaculate suede shoes.

'What are you doing here?' she demanded breathlessly, all social pretence abandoned.

He lifted one shoulder in a wry shrug.

'I told you I wanted to see you—what was your

cousin's phrase—without interruptions? I don't think we're likely to be interrupted now, do you?'

Philippa glared at him. 'I suppose you think that's funny.'

Raoul tipped his head on one side and allowed that slow smile that she dreaded to grow.

'That's right. I think it's very amusing.'

She resisted the temptation to throw the soaking sponge at him.

'Well, I don't. Get out,' she told him crisply.

His eyes wandered over her. She knew what he was seeing: the pale skin faintly tanned after her days in the sun, the droplets of bathwater making it glimmer like gossamer, smooth, gleaming shoulders and tip tilted breasts that revealed, to her profound shame, the effect his unexpected appearance had had on her. She wanted to cringe away, to hide, to become invisible. But it was impossible and pride came to her aid. She lifted her chin and met his eyes squarely.

His mouth twisted mockingly.

'You get more beautiful every time I see you,' he told her lightly.

The cool, indifferent tone made it almost an insult. Philippa whitened. The lack of feeling there cut at her like a slashing sword. It was exactly the sort of casually flirtatious remark he would make to a woman with whom he was having a passing affair. All the jet-setting ladies, Rupert had said, she thought painfully. And that was exactly how Raoul treated her, expecting her to enjoy the compatibility between his body and her own. Only she could not forget that he despised her. Sometimes he seemed almost to hate her.

Though she did not know it, the green eyes darkened. For a moment she looked inexpressibly sad. Raoul's brows twitched together in a frown.

'What have I said now?' he demanded impatiently.

She swallowed. 'Nothing.'

'I don't understand you,' he exclaimed. 'Most women like compliments.'

Philippa looked away. 'I suppose I don't see—that—as a compliment,' she said with difficulty.

The fine brows rose incredulously. 'Not to be told you are beautiful? You have high standards in compliments,' Raoul said sardonically.

She made a helpless gesture. 'They're only words.'

She had not meant to sound aggressive but that was the way it came out. There was a taut silence. Raoul stared at her broodingly, his face set in harsh lines and quite unreadable.

Then he said softly. 'So you don't trust words?'

She shook her head. She could not speak. If only he would stop standing there so close and yet so inaccessible. It was all she could do not to cry out and beg him to take her in his arms and make love to her, no matter what the consequences.

That would be disastrous. He would break her. Already other people were discovering her foolish, futile love. If Rupert had found her out, how long would it be before Raoul, so much more acute, became aware that he was the unwilling object of her love?

'You may be right,' he said thoughtfully, still in that soft chilling voice. He gave her a smile that did not touch his eyes, like an enemy advancing to victory. 'Words have never done that much for us. They say action speaks louder, though up to now you have given no sign of preferring it. Still, if you've changed your mind . . .' The smile was now definitely unpleasant. 'Come here.'

For a moment she did not understand him. Then, as his meaning dawned, her eyes widened.

'No,' she gasped in a choked voice.

Even pride was not strong enough to prevent her

reaching out clumsily for the fluffy towel. She stood up, pulling it round her with hands that shook, scrambling out of the bath in undignified haste.

There was a bell push in the corner beyond the hand basin and she dashed over to it and pushed it wildly. Raoul watched her, making no attempt to intercept, apparently deriving a good deal of amusement from her proceedings. Philippa faced him, panting.

'*Now* will you get out? Henriette will be here in a minute.'

He laughed. 'I doubt that.' He leant back against the edge of the basin, his hands in his trouser pockets, his eyes glinting down at her.

'Henriette is busy. She knows I am up here. She will think that if you are in any dire straits I will come to your assistance. As,' he said gently, 'I shall.'

There was no mistaking his intentions.

Philippa closed her eyes and said in despair, 'Please don't. I can't bear it. Please. Oh please, no.'

She was still murmuring in distress when he picked her up. He paid no attention, striding back into the bedroom and tossing her on to the bed with almost contemptuous ease. She lay there, her eyes tight shut, shaking with the effort of not reaching for him, not pouring out all her unwanted love.

Raoul said cruelly, 'You know, if I didn't know different, I would say you were frigid.'

Her eyes flew open. He smiled down at her, at his most sardonic. He was unbuttoning his shirt. When he flung it away from him, her mouth went dry and her whole body clenched in trepidation. The watchful eyes noted it, without the least sign of relenting. He stripped unhurriedly, his eyes never leaving her face.

'That's a pretty good imitation of it, you've got there,' he said conversationally. 'The shrinking bride, mark three, new improved model.'

'I loathe you,' Philippa said in a shaking voice, consumed with shame.

'That,' Raoul said with sudden savagery, 'is obvious.'

He flung himself down beside her, naked and powerful, divesting her of the frail protection of the towel with ruthless determination. Philippa could not bear it. She thrust the palms of her hands against her eyes, so that all she could see were swirls of blackness, blotting out his fierce face, his tanned, terrifying body.

'Oh no,' said the hateful voice. 'You don't hide from me or yourself like that.'

Her hands were seized and pushed down hard at her sides. She was subjected to a slow and deliberate scrutiny which made her burn with humiliation. She dragged against his hold but he hardly seemed to notice it, holding her still as his eyes travelled over her.

When he had finished, the eyes, hard as diamonds, came back to her flushed face. His mouth was a thin line. He looked reckless, dangerous. For a moment Philippa had the feeling that, in spite of that insulting inspection, he was not really seeing her at all but some demon out of his own imaginings. He had an oddly bitter look as if he had been hurt. Which was ridiculous because the only person likely to be hurt was herself. Nevertheless, she felt compassion stir and, forgetting briefly her own panic, she stared at him in concern.

'Raoul . . .' she began gently.

His gaze sharpened, slid back to her and the present; the brooding look disappeared.

'Yes, darling,' he said, the endearment a mockery.

She flinched but met his eyes bravely.

'Raoul, don't—*please* don't—do something which will hurt both of us.'

He put back his head and laughed at that.

'You're not going to get hurt darling. You know the mark three model is only reluctant up to a point.'

He was unreachable. She could not deflect him. His hands, no longer pinning her wrists to her sides, were moving on her body with absolute mastery and she was overwhelmed with delight. Her breath was coming faster, her eyes misting.

'Isn't it?' he insisted.

He levered himself up on to one elbow and looked down at her. Philippa thought she had never seen such a scornful expression on anyone's face before.

'No,' she said, begging him not to look like that, not to despise her.

The expression vanished. His face became a mask. And very, very slowly he began to stroke his thumb backwards and forwards against the underside of her breast. Philippa's breath caught in her throat, knowing she was helpless to suppress the surge of feeling which had her body arching up to his hands.

'No?' he said in bitter mockery, pausing for an agonising instant, before he took her offered flesh into his domination.

Phillipa felt as if she were travelling at high speed, so high that all her body, blood and bones and nerves, were liquifying, turning to molten gold, to sunlight. She was no longer herself. She was another creature, Raoul's creature, he was her only fellow, the other half of herself. Her face was wet with tears, though she did not know that she had been crying. Her ears were full of the sound of rushing water, of all that melting sunlight.

And in her ear, in her brain, her very heart's core, she heard Raoul say, on a shaken half-laugh, 'Now!' She tensed, only half comprehending, and then, like some missile flung from a catapult, she felt herself pierced, exploding, shattering on impact into a million untraceable fragments. And among all the scattered pieces of herself a great, grief-stricken silence fell.

So he has finally destroyed me, Philippa thought, almost without emotion. There could be no doubts left now. He might not care for her but he was a man of considerable experience. He would know that he sent her up in flames and he would know why. She was in such despair that she hardly even felt shame.

He rolled away from her, not speaking, his own breathing returning slowly to normal. She was grateful that he did not say anything. She could not have lied in reply and she did not think that she could bear the truth; to admit she loved him to his face was more than she could endure. She did not know what would be worse: his embarrassment or his kind, careless sympathy.

Philippa turned her head softly and found that Raoul, his head thrown back in an attitude of abandoned relaxation, had fallen asleep. For a moment she was startled. In spite of her misery, she could not forbear to smile. Her feelings, her self-respect, her whole life had been shattered by his hands and, serenely unconscious that anything out of the ordinary had taken place, Raoul drifted off into a snooze.

She left him, stealthily. She went back to the bathroom, pulled the plug, gave the bath a perfunctory clean, dressed, arranged her hair, applied make-up with a hand that was astonishingly steady. When she was as perfectly groomed as she could achieve, she straightened her shoulders and went back into the bedroom to face him.

Raoul had gone. The double doors to his room where half open, as if he had pushed them apart impatiently. She could not see him but she heard him clearly enough. He might have been talking to Gerard or, then again, he might have been on the telephone. It was odd that she was sure that it was neither of those.

He sounded wry, a little weary. 'I haven't,' he was

saying, 'had a chance to broach the subject. She was not in a receptive mood.' He gave an impatient sigh. 'You'll just have to do your best. Talk to her yourself.'

Too grateful that he was engaged to pay much attention to what he was saying, Philippa went to the door and slipped noiselessly out into the corridor. The door to Raoul's room was open and, standing just in the lee of it, she could make out the figure of a man, casually dressed in jeans and checked shirt. It was not Rupert. It was not anyone she had ever met before.

She met him at dinner. His name was Alex Januar and he seemed to be some sort of substitute escort for Sally Sebastian. Raoul, true to his word, had invited guests to amuse him during the weekend and Sally had been his choice. She sat next to him, flirting her eyelashes, teasing him, pouting when he teased her in his turn while Rupert glared and Philippa sat in an icy calm, not hearing more than one word in three that Monsieur Januar addressed to her.

The meal was perfectly cooked. It was also perfectly served by a glacial Gerard. Philippa wondered whether he had told Raoul about Rupert's early arrival and if that was what had brought her husband home. But no, it was impossible. Raoul must have set out on the road even before Rupert left Bordeaux.

Still, Gerard might have said something to Raoul. Her husband was treating her with a cool courtesy that he might equally well have used to an unfamiliar business acquaintance. You would never have guessed that he had dredged such passionate abandon from her less than an hour earlier. He did not refer to it by so much as a look.

Though he did say, when she snatched her hand away from his when their fingers met accidentally as they both reached for the coffee pot, 'I see that the mark three model is back with us.'

It must have been a trick of the candle flung shadows that made him look uncharacteristically tired when he spoke. For a moment, Philippa was moved by his expression of defeat but then she met Rupert's eyes, watchful and sympathetic, across the table and realised she was about to make a fool of herself yet again.

So she pretended not to have heard, turning her attention to Monsieur Januar and giving a very creditable performance of listening to him with attention.

She went to bed early leaving them all with their wine. Nobody questioned her statement that she was tired and one look in her mirror when she got back to her room showed her why. Beneath her light tan she was colourless. Her eyes were enormous and faintly dazed, as if she were in shock. So the strain, she thought grimly, was beginning to show.

She wondered what Raoul would say when he came to bed. Would he mock her for being hollow eyed, discerning the cause? Or would he be impatient? More likely, he would ignore her protests and the silent signs of her distress alike, she thought. If he could abandon her, ignore her, spend an afternoon obliquely putting her in her place and then, presumably because it momentarily pleased him to do so, make love to her, he was not likely to take much notice of anything she did or said.

She went out on to the balcony. The air was full of the scent of the jasmine under her window. It reminded her sharply of her uncle's garden. Tears pricked her eyes.

I shall have to leave him, she thought. I shall have to go back to England and put myself together again before it becomes completely impossible. If I stay, I'll turn into a zombie, alive only when Raoul is here. And feeling, only when you're in his arms, added an unwelcome inner voice.

Philippa pressed her hands to her cheeks. Why pretend? Even if she ran away now, there would be no escape for her. Raoul had already made her his, and only his, in every important way.

What's wrong with me, she thought. Am I a slave? Have I no will of my own? Am I going to surrender my whole life because he moves me physically? A great deal more than physically, said that inexorable voice: or why else do you want to comfort him when he seems defeated, hold him when he is bitter? You're in love with a man who has no use for love. The sooner you go the better, but you know you won't. As long as you can do anything for him at all, you will stay and hope against hope that he learns to love you.

It was a chilling prospect. It meant that she awaited Raoul torn between returning excitement and flat despair. It also meant that she stayed awake all night. Because, inexplicably, unpredictably, he did not come.

Nor, as she had good reason to know, having spent a sleepless night waiting for the sound of his door or the sight of a light under the connecting doors between their rooms, did he sleep in his own bed. She finally fell asleep, as dawn touched the horizon, knowing that the room next to her own was unoccupied.

CHAPTER ELEVEN

On Saturday morning Raoul took his guests riding, dragging a reluctant Rupert with him. He refused, however, to allow Philippa to go.

'You'd probably fall off,' he told her bluntly. 'Which would be a nuisance.' And then, nastily, 'You'll see Rupert at lunch.'

She ignored that. 'I ride reasonably well,' she protested.

'Perhaps. But have you ever ridden after a bad accident? For God's sake take a look at yourself,' Raoul said impatiently. 'You're a wreck. The best thing you can do is go back to bed.'

She did not, though. After they had all ridden out, Sally Sebastian looking crisp and healthy in cream twill trousers and a cotton shirt which she said laughingly belonged to her brother, Philippa went to the pool and swam its length grimly. She did it over and over again until her arms were so tired and heavy that she could hardly lift them. Then she got out of the water and collapsed on to one of the loungers. She was asleep in seconds.

When she awoke, it was to feel fingers running lightly over her shoulders. She tensed at once, instantly alert, and flipped over on her back with a protest on her lips. Only to meet her cousin's surprised expression.

'You thought it was Raoul, didn't you?' he demanded. When she didn't answer he said, 'What on earth has he done to you to make you jump like a rabbit?'

Philippa recovered herself.

'Not a thing. I thought there were ants walking over me,' she said calmly. 'There's lots of them about and they give me the horrors.'

Rupert looked sceptical but did not pursue the subject. Instead he talked about Sally Sebastian, how she had changed, how she was so pushy and aggressive, how she flirted with Raoul all the time.

Philippa steeled herself. 'She's very attractive. She's got every right to enjoy men's admiration.'

Rupert was dissatisfied. 'She's keeps boasting about what a successful professional woman she is, as if that gives her the right to do anything she wants, no matter how inconsiderate. You were a successful professional woman; you didn't behave like that.'

'I don't care for the past tense,' Philippa said mildly. 'I'm only lazing about here because I'm convalescent. When I'm better I shall go back to work.'

Rupert laughed. 'That's not what Raoul says.'

'What?' She was too surprised even to attempt to disguise her astonishment.

'He was telling Sally this morning,' said Rupert, unaware of undercurrents. 'Teasing her, you know. Saying that if she got a man of her own she'd have to do what you've done and leave the independent life behind. The implication was that you'd start having children at once. Sally,' added Rupert with incomprehensible satisfaction, 'was as mad as fire about it, Told him he was a male chauvinist pig . . .'

He broke off, as a long shadow fell across them.

'Do I recognise myself?' said Raoul, amused.

Philippa's throat felt stiff. She gave him a small, uncertain smile and then averted her gaze to look across the ruffled water of the pool. Even without looking at him, she knew he was smiling. A slow fury began to rise in her. How could he smile, after the events of yesterday? How *dared* he smile, having spent the night away from his own room? Had he been with Sally? There was no way to tell from the impeturbable, smiling mask.

Jealousy was poison. Feeling it eat its way along her nerves, Philippa acknowledged it grimly. She didn't know whether her husband was having an affair with Sally Sebastian. Reason told her not. It would be unnecessarily foolhardy to bring the girl home and introduce her to his wife if he was having an affair with her. And Raoul was not foolhardy.

But in spite of the logic of the thing, she was consumed with jealousy just on the suspicion of their being lovers. Without evidence, without even a good argument to support her suspicions, she was half way convinced already.

Rupert and Raoul were talking, in the barbed, polite way of men who mistrust each other but she barely heard a word they said. Her whole being was concentrated, waiting for the moment when Sally appeared. Surely then she would be able to tell—from Raoul's expression, from Sally's manner to him, from what they said, or what they did not, she thought in anguish.

'. . . Pipps?' Rupert was saying.

She jumped. 'Oh, I'm sorry. I wasn't listening. What were you saying?'

Raoul gave her his most false and charming smile.

'Your cousin wanted to know whether you were coming to buy wine with us this afternoon. I said that I was sure you would prefer to stay here. You can show Alex round the grounds, as you promised to do last night.

He wants to be alone with Sally, Philippa thought numbly, but she said, 'D-did I? I'd forgotten. But of course I must if I've promised.'

'Good,' said Raoul heartily. For a moment he looked

positively mischievous. 'I like a woman who keeps her promises,' he murmured, and raised her cold hand to his lips.

Philippa gave a sudden uncontrollable shudder, as if that mocking touch had set up a electrical current through her body. She snatched her hand away, scrambling to her feet.

'I'll see about lunch,' she said distractedly, ignoring the black frown which had descended on Raoul's brow.

She fled from the pool and managed, by dint of a ferocious bustle of housewifely activities, to keep out of Raoul's way even during the casual lunch on the terrace. She would have been happy enough to keep away from Alex Januar as well but he held her to her forgotten promise.

So she escorted him round the formal gardens and the meadowland, making stilted conversation which carefully skirted any mention of her husband or his fellow guest. In fact it was only when they got on to the subject of the local wild flowers, on which she was becoming an expert, that Philippa felt herself relax. Alex Januar knew a surprising amount about landscape but not, she found about individual plants and, provided they steered well clear of any discussion of personalities, she found herself enjoying her conversation with him more than she would have believed possible. He was one of Raoul's jet-setting friends, of course. He was as cool and sophisticated as Raoul himself in some ways. But his interest in the gardens was genuine enough and he seemed happy to discuss plants without any of that edged mockery that she so dreaded in Raoul.

It was a relief to find him so easy a guest. Compared with Rupert's edgy temper and Sally Sebastian's evident intimacy with Raoul, Alex Januar's company was blissfully uncomplicated. It hurt, just a little, to see

Raoul encouraging her tête-à-têtes with his guest because he was presumably doing so in order to allow himself more time alone with Sally. Rupert clearly thought so, glaring at Alex and Philippa in their corner after dinner.

'You're playing into his hands,' he hissed at her, as he refilled his brandy glass.

Philippa looked up from the book of flower prints she was showing Alex.

'What are you talking about?'

Rupert looked furious. 'Come out on the terrace and I'll tell you.'

Alex seemed unaware of the exchange, absorbed in the book. She hesitated, looking at his downbent head, and then with a small murmur got up and followed Rupert to the french windows. Raoul, who had been smiling approvingly, suddenly glared and, thought Philippa, aware of his every move without looking at him, made as if to rise. Sally put out an elegantly manicured hand and touched his arm. Raoul subsided.

Outside the air was as warm as it had been by day, warmer than the shuttered room they had just left. Rupert was little more than a shadow, leaning against the balustrade like a passenger on a liner staring out over the ocean.

'What is it?' said Philippa to his romantic profile.

She was wary but a little amused also. Rupert liked to dramatise things, and never more so than when he was in the centre of the stage. He did not look at her but extracted a cigarette from his case and lit it with quick, angry puffs.

'You know he's got Januar down here deliberately?' he said in a hasty tone, as if he disliked what he had to say.

'Deliberately?' Philippa echoed, not understanding.

'For you.'

She shook her head slowly. 'I don't know what you're getting at.'

'To chat you up. To seduce you.' And as she still stared at him in silence he said brutally, 'To get you into bed, for God's sake.'

Her first thought was that Rupert had allowed his taste for drama to go to far. She said with dignity. 'That's a stupid thing to say Rupert and in foul taste, even for you.'

She turned to go back inside but he stopped her, not by touching her but by saying in a miserable voice like an unhappy schoolboy, 'I'm awfully sorry, Pipps. I wish it wasn't true. But I heard him——' he swallowed audibly. 'I heard him telling Januar what to do. He told him he'd get him the opportunity to be alone with you this afternoon. And he did, didn't he?'

Philippa put out a hand and hung on to the back of one of the cane terrace chairs for support.

'I don't believe it,' she said passionately.

He did not answer, smoking with jerky movements.

'I don't *believe* it.'

Rupert shrugged.

'But—why?' she said, almost pleading with him to deny it.

He shifted against the balustrade, pitching the cigarette away from him. She saw the red tip arc high before it fell to be extinguished on the gravel path beneath them.

'Sally says . . .'

'Sally?' Philippa was sharp. 'You've discussed this with Sally Sebastian?'

'God, no,' said Rupert with feeling. 'She's been talking to me, though. Did you know you cut her out with de Martin? I don't know whether she thought he would marry her,' he said bitterly, 'but she sure as hell didn't expect him to marry anyone else. She was furious and she's been nagging him about it. And apparently he told her——' he passed a hand over his eyes briefly. 'Look, you don't want to hear this, Pipps. It'll only upset you. Just take my word for it.'

'Tell me,' she said in a quiet voice.

'But . . .'

'Tell me.'

'That Bob was right. That you were frigid. That he'd married you on the understanding that you would both go your own ways and you weren't keeping your side of the bargain. That you hadn't ever had a love affair and weren't likely to do so in the future because you were— well—disgusted by the idea of sex,' Rupert said in a rush. 'Sally said she sympathised with him. It sort of tied him down in a way he hadn't bargained for. So they put their heads together and came up with Alex Januar as the man to, well, to . . .'

'Get their consciences off the hook?' asked Philippa, still in that deadly calm voice.

'I suppose you could put it like that,' Rupert said unhappily. 'I wouldn't have believed her, Pipps, honestly I wouldn't. But then I heard Januar talking to him this morning, and it all made sense.'

'Yes,' she agreed.

Somewhere inside her a great anger was building up. She could recall vividly Raoul smiling benignly down the dinner table at them, encouraging her to show Alex the result of her research, arranging for her to take him round the grounds. And all with the one cynical objective of launching her on an affair which would serve to justify his own.

Very slowly she released the back of the chair and stepped away from it.

'What are you going to do?' asked Rupert in obvious alarm.

'Murder has its attractions,' said Philippa between her teeth.

He moved quickly and took her shoulders between his hands and held her still.

'Don't rush into anything,' he urged. 'Not something you'll later regret. If you go steaming in there now, he'll tear you apart. You're no match for him, Pipps. He's a shrewd bastard and he can make black look white if he wants. Look how he's got Sally playing his game,' he added bitterly.

'Sally?' For the first time it occurred to Philippa that Rupert was showing unwonted interest in the activities of a woman who did not appear to have fallen head over heels in love with him.

'I've been mad about her for years,' Rupert said roughly. 'That's why I hoped you and Bob would get it together. Why I was so angry when you didn't.'

Philippa stood very still. It was odd, she thought in a detached way, she had been desperately unhappy about Bob Sebastian and his rough handling of her. It had haunted her for years, not least because the Vivians had been out of sympathy with her. Now, she found, she did not care any more.

Bob was no more than an unpleasant memory. The only person with the power to hurt her now was her husband. And he had done so. When she stopped being angry, she thought, she would find out how much of her he had destroyed and what there was left to build a new, devastated life. Not a great deal, she imagined. She stirred her anger. It was better by far to be angry with him than to despair. If she could only stay angry until she got out of his home and his country, she might be able to salvage a little self respect.

She said remotely, 'Tough.'

'Oh, she won't look at me. She never has done. I'm

not the dynamic, successful type. I'm not in the de
Martin league any more than you are.'

She gave a little choke of laughter then, though it
broke in the middle. Rupert pulled her roughly against
his chest, patting her hair awkwardly.

'You can't go on with it,' he said urgently. 'You've
got to get away from him, Pipps.' And, in a sudden
rush of generosity. 'I'll take you away from him.'

She was surprised and would have said so but she did
not have time. The french window was sent crashing
back on its hinges and a quick step on the paved terrace
made her break apart from Rupert and swing round.

'You,' said Raoul with ferocious control, 'will do
nothing of the sort. If you value your pampered life you
will get back into the salon and keep out of my way.
You have tried my patience long enough.'

But Rupert, too, was at the end of his tether.

'I won't,' he snarled. 'And I'll get Pipps away from
you if it's the last thing I do.'

He made a clumsy lunge at Raoul which was parried
with a quick, vicious blow. Rupert crumpled, groaning.

'Get up,' Raoul told him contemptuously. 'You're
not hurt.'

Rupert hauled himself to his feet though he was
plainly in too much pain to straighten up. He had both
arms huddled protectively over his stomach as if in
anticipation of another blow. Philippa stepped forward.

'Stop it! she said crisply. 'I will not have you brawling
like children.'

'I'll get you away,' Rupert said groggily, clinging to
his chivalrous impulse very creditably.

She softened. 'We'll talk about it tomorrow. For
heaven's sake go and get your breath back now. I want
to talk to——' she had nearly said my husband; she bit
her lip, '—to Raoul.'

Rupert went, watched enigmatically by Raoul.

Philippa was shaken with a gust of white hot fury. She would wipe the smile off those handsome, cynical features, she promised herself. She composed herself, trying for an air of indifference.

'Impressive,' she told him mockingly. 'I didn't realise you went in for sparring matches with your guests.'

He ignored that. 'What were you doing out here with him?'

She lifted one shoulder carelessly. 'Admiring the stars,' she offered in a flippant tone.

He took a step forward as if he could barely control himself.

'What is this business about taking you away?'

Philippa gave a soft laugh. 'Yes, that gets you on the raw, doesn't it? You're not keen on losing your possessions.'

Raoul was very still. 'Possession?'

'Isn't that what I am?' In spite of her determination, the pain and anger were beginning to show through.

Raoul said slowly, 'You're my wife.'

'I am indeed,' she said bitterly. 'Signed, sealed delivered, not covered by guarantee in event of non-performance. How soon will you decide that I'm not the wife you bargained for and cancel the contract Raoul? And when you do, will you still revenge yourself on Vivians? Or is the company safe now that it's part of your empire?'

Her angry words fell into a pool of silence. Raoul said nothing. Nor had he moved. It was as if he had turned into a statue in the dusk. Philippa shivered: a statue she could batter herself to death against. She dragged hard on the rags of her anger: if she let them go she would start to feel sorry for herself and then Raoul would have every last weapon in his hands.

She said harshly, 'Did you bring Alex Januar here to

. . .' she floundered, not knowing how to express it, 'for me?' she ended.

He sounded faintly surprised. 'Of course.'

She had thought she was hurt before but it was nothing to the sickening pain that shot through her now. Just that little, casual phrase and her last hope was crushed to powder. For a moment she could not speak.

Then she swallowed the obstruction in her throat.

'Why didn't you tell me?' she said in little more than a whisper. 'Why just spring Alex on me? Couldn't we have talked about it?'

Raoul said coolly, 'I was pretty sure you would resist the idea. I thought the less time you had to think about it the more likely he was to persuade you.'

'He!' Philippa was scornful. 'He couldn't care less and you know it.'

'Not to begin with, no. That has to be true. But he tells me he is getting more excited about it by the moment.'

The anger exploded, quite suddenly, in glorious rocketing fury.

'How good of him,' she said affably. 'And how good of you to tell me.' Her eyes were glittering; her voice sank to a fierce undertone. 'I would not have believed it possible that anyone would dare to do or say what you have done. I tried to keep my side of the bargain, even though I never wanted it in the first place. But you—you have abused the contract, taken advantage of me at every turn. When Rupert leaves tomorrow I shall go with him and the only way you will stop me is by force. Is that clear?'

She was panting with the violence of her emotions. Raoul, by contrast, was perfectly cool.

'And all this is because of poor old Alex?' he demanded incredulously.

For a horrifying moment Philippa thought she would hit him, faint, throw back her head and scream her outrage to the moon. She was shaking like a tree in a hurricane. She pressed her palms together, steadying herself.

'Alex,' she said with difficulty, 'is the last straw. Though I can quite see that you do not understand what a gross insult you have offered me.'

'Insult?' Raoul sounded amused, impatient, irritated. 'My dear girl, it's a compliment.'

She did hit him then, instinctively, without timing her blow or thinking of anything but the raging humiliation that stormed through her. Raoul was unprepared and flinched back, half falling until he put out a hand to save himself against the balustrade. He braced himself there, as if it was only by a superhuman effort of will that he restrained himself from laying violent hands on her.

But Philippa was not frightened. She had gone beyond fear of self-consciousness. She only knew that while, in other circumstances she loved this man to distraction and would do so till she died, just at the moment she would cheerfully have tipped him into the rose garden's fountain.

'*You* may think so,' she said in a low voice which cut like a whip. 'It does not surprise me. I do not intend to argue with you. I can only tell you that it is the last—and worst—of the cruel insults you have heaped on me. And,' she added with a last flash of fire, 'I shall never forgive you for any of them.'

CHAPTER TWELVE

IT was late when Philippa's secretary buzzed through to her on their intercommunicating telephone. The late autumn weather was golden during the day but it grew dark early. She had been working by the light of her desk lamp for more than an hour.

'Yes, Karen?' she asked, flicking the communicator switch on her machine.

'Mr Vivian's secretary rang to say that he's not feeling well and is going home,' Karen reported. She was a nice girl and a good secretary, usually friendly as a sparrow. Now she sounded oddly formal. 'He wants you to take the monthly meeting.'

'Me?' Philippa frowned, drawing circles round the new design for a perfume bottle that she had been studying. 'But can't Tim go?'

'He is going,' Karen sounded even more stilted. 'But I gather Mr Vivian was most insistent that you should accompany him to talk about the projections.'

Philippa sighed. Horribly, it made sense. Up to now her uncle, who had been uncomplainingly kind to her on her return from France, had aided and abetted her in her avoidance of any meeting where she would come across Martin Industries executives. Today he was presumably not able to help himself.

'What's in my diary, Karen?'

Her secretary read off a couple of appointments, neither of them important. She could not honestly say that it was imperative that she keep either.

'Mmm,' she said, still musing, still reluctant. 'And have you got a copy of the agenda? And a list of other people attending?'

'Yes, Miss Carr,' said Karen, even more subdued.

Philippa's eyes narrowed and her pen-tip on the paper began to score deep gouges. Karen used her christian name except in front of clients. Nobody had ever called her by her married name, of course.

'Bring them in, will you,' she asked, and closed the communication channel.

Karen appeared almost immediately her cheeks flushed and looking much more discomposed than Philippa had ever seen her. She stared.

She put down the pages in front of Philippa and leant across the desk.

'He's outside in my office,' she hissed. 'He says he wants to see you. Now. And I'm not to tell you who's here.'

Philippa felt her mouth to go dry. She did not need to ask who. She looked down a little blindly at the top paper and saw clearly that the accredited representative from the parent company at this evening's meeting was Comte Raoul de Martin. She was conscious of a craven desire to run.

She said, 'Does he know I'm here?'

Karen was almost weeping with mortification. 'Yes. I'm sorry. It was he who told me to ring Mr Vivian's secretary. And then he stood over me while I spoke to you. I didn't know what to do.'

'It's not your fault,' said Philippa automatically. Her smile was a little twisted. 'He can be very difficult to— withstand.' She put a hand to the back of her neck, feeling the tension there and knowing that nothing she could do would ease it. 'And he wants to see me now?'

Karen nodded, distressed.

'Well then I'd better see him, hadn't I?' She closed her eyes for a second, trying to calm her pulses and failing. 'How long before the meeting starts?'

Karen gestured to the paper. 'Fifteen minutes in theory. Monsieur de Martin is to chair it. It will wait for him.'

'No doubt. But I can at least insist that he starts on time.' A wintery smile touched the corners of her mouth, leaving her eyes bleak. 'Give me three minutes to tidy myself, Karen and then show him in.'

Subdued the girl nodded and went out. She was fond of Philippa for whom she had worked ever since she rejoined the firm on her return from France. There had been a good deal of speculation of course about what had happened to her marriage. Philippa's previous secretary, now working for the finance director, had said, shocked, that she was like a ghost of her former self. She had lost weight, there were great shadows under her eyes, and, though she was always pleasant, when she thought no one was looking at her she wore an expression of absolute despair.

To Karen, who was new to the firm, all this was unverifiable. What she did know about was the work. Philippa was at her desk before anyone but the janitor had arrived in the building. And she was there late into the night, leaving, preoccupied and hollow-eyed, only when dispossessed by the late night cleaners. And she frequently took work home with her, as Karen, who typed the notes dictated at home the night before, had good reason to know.

She did not seem to have any private life at all. She barely saw her uncle and never went to stay with him and his wife in the country, though she had gone often enough before her marriage. She went to the opera sometimes, though always with a party of friends rather than a single male companion. And if men did ring her up to ask her to lunch or dinner or the theatre, she always turned them down.

Karen, a romantic, had hoped that it was because she

was desperately in love with her husband from whom circumstances had unavoidably parted her. But this was clearly not the case. He never rang or wrote. And, though everybody knew he was in London because he was photographed at the airport, he made no attempt that she could discover to get in touch with his wife.

Karen did not know that Philippa had seen that photograph over a man's shoulder in the underground and gone cold with panic. She had given orders that she was busy and not to be disturbed, all her telephone calls were to be routed through her secretary, nobody was to be allowed into her suite of offices without her prior consent. And she had left early, for once, hailing a taxi to take her home just in case Raoul—foolish thought—had decided to lurk at the underground station and catch up with her there. When she got home she took the 'phone off the hook and, though the entryphone buzzer to her block of flats rang three times, she had not answered it.

Raoul, if he had indeed tried to contact her, had been successfully discouraged. There was a businesslike letter about a settlement which she had immediately turned over to her lawyer with instructions that she wanted no allowance or anything else from Raoul. As soon as she could find another job, she told him to inform her husband, she would leave Vivian Glass and then they would have no further contact, which was what she earnestly desired.

Finding another job was not hard. Persuading Uncle David that she was dispensable was another matter. With Rupert gone and Raoul's high powered executives appointed to his Board, David Vivian was feeling old and frail and in need of all the support he could get. In the end Philippa had not the heart to leave him in the lurch.

She did, however, establish that she should never be required to have anything to do with the parent company or its Chief Executive. Uncle David, much inclined to play Cupid, had acquiesced but invited her down to Shropshire for the weekend when, though he had not told her so, Raoul was expected. Philippa had found it out by pure chance because she had stopped in the village to fill up with petrol and was treated by the garage owner, whom she had known from childhood, to an admiring dissertation on the glorious Mercedes that he had in for a check up. Philippa, taken to inspect it, found she knew the car. It did not take the French nationality plates to make her suspect who was driving it.

She had turned her own car round and returned to London. On arrival she had telephoned her aunt and said, with chilling and unmistakable resolution, that she did not intend to visit them again since they had played such a trick on her. And would they please refrain from doing anything similar again—or she would leave Vivians at once.

That had been six weeks ago, after which it had all subsided. Uncle David was hurt and took care to show it but Philippa ignored him and they were both too busy to spend time on reproaches. From Raoul there was silence.

Until today. Philippa, pulled a comb through her untidy hair, drew several sustaining deep breaths. The one thing he must have relied on was that she would not be so unfair as to expose her secretary to his displeasure. Therefore his approach to her in office hours. As strategy it was faultless, and showed a reading of her character that she found equally shrewd and worrying.

She bit her lip, straightened her shoulders and buzzed Karen.

'You can show Monsieur de Martin in now, Karen,' she said quietly.

Raoul came in softly like a watchful cat. Philippa could not suppress the first instinctive shiver of apprehension at the sight of him, even though she was prepared. But she took hold of herself and stood up behind her desk. For a moment they stood quite still, viewing each other like adversaries. Then he smiled.

'This is an honour I was beginning to suspect I would never achieve,' he drawled, his mocking eyes not leaving her face.

She put up her brows. 'You must know I would not have told my secretary to throw you out.'

'Yes, but you would have liked to, wouldn't you?'

He strolled forward and sat himself, very much at his ease, on the linen-covered sofa by the window.

'What do you want?' she said abruptly.

His eyes narrowed. 'A hearing. Even a condemned man is entitled to that.'

'I don't want to talk to you,' she said brusquely.

Raoul smiled with no apparent mirth. 'You have made that abundantly clear. I, however, want to talk to you.'

She shrugged. 'Tough,' she told him in a hard voice.

'And I'm prepared to sit here until I've finished,' he went on imperturbably. 'And,' intercepting her glance at the door, 'to make sure that you do the same.'

'You have a meeting in,' she consulted her watch, 'eleven minutes. If you want to sit here for eleven minutes, I shan't try to stop you.'

He crossed one leg over the other with an air of perfect relaxation. Warily, Philippa resumed her seat and pulled the minutes of the previous meeting towards her. It was impossible that she could concentrate, of course, with him sitting there studying her, but she could try.

'I don't intend to go to that meeting, you know,' Raoul said at last conversationally.

'What?' She jumped, her eyes flying to meet his. 'But it says here——' and she gestured helplessly at the papers in her hand.

He nodded. 'Yes.'

'But is the meeting cancelled, then? I was supposed to be going to it.'

'The meeting is not cancelled. Everyone else will go. You and I will not.'

'But that's stupid,' Philippa protested. 'And rude. It's a terrible waste of everybody's time.' Slowly the full import of what he had said dawned on her. She glared at him in dawning dismay. 'And they'll all sit round the table wondering where you and I are.'

He nodded pleasantly. 'Quite.'

She said between her teeth. 'You're despicable. You're using my position as your professional subordinate against me. You don't even play fair.'

His mouth was wry. 'At this stage I need every advantage I can get, fair or not.'

Philippa clenched her hands impotently.

'There is an alternative of course,' he pursued gently. 'I could go to the meeting as arranged. You could even accompany me. And then you would come back to my hotel suite for dinner and—for once—give me a fair hearing. Or we stay here. It's up to you.'

Once again, Philippa realised, she had been outmanoeuvred by a master strategist.

'I don't want to have dinner with you,' she said trying for dignity and sounding like a sulky child.

His lips twitched. 'There is no minimum consumption required. If you don't want to eat, then of course you need not. But you have got to *listen*!'

She hesitated, resentful and indecisive. Her intercom buzzed.

'Your meeting, Miss Carr,' Karen's most formal voice reminded her.

Raoul, in his corner, stretched his arms high above his head and laughed.

'Damn you,' said Philippa in concentrated fury. 'You win.'

He bowed his head in acknowledgment. 'Of course.'

She showed her teeth. 'This round,' she promised him. 'Only this round.'

He stood up, a hand out for her papers before he motioned her, with an elaborate courtesy of which she was highly suspicious, to precede him through the door.

'Of course,' he said again ironically. 'I only fight one round at a time.'

Philippa hardly heard what was said at the meeting. She contributed not at all. Raoul, on the other hand, infuriatingly calm and efficient, chaired the meeting with economy, got a number of decisions endorsed, commissioned two further studies, one from Philippa's department and brought the meeting to a close in under an hour.

'It's probably a record,' Philippa said sourly as one of the design directors commented on Raoul's command.

'He certainly doesn't hang about,' he agreed. Then, looking between Raoul who was chatting to the finance director and Philippa, he pursed his lips in a soundless whistle. 'Guess he's got somewhere better to go and something better to do,' he observed teasingly.

Philippa, to her fury, went scarlet. Across the room Raoul observed it, as she saw very clearly when she raised her eyes from her portfolio. His face was the smooth mask she knew so well but she also knew that underneath the calm exterior he was enjoying himself enormously at her expense. He strolled across to her.

'Coming, darling?' he asked, not bothering to lower his voice.

She set her teeth.

'I have to collect my coat.'

'I'll wait for you in the lobby,' he said, a faint note of warning in his voice.

He need not have bothered, she thought. She would not try to evade him by slipping out of the back entrance. He had probably posted sentries there, and she would achieve was her own embarrassment.

The best she could hope for this evening was to hear whatever he had to say and keep the temperature low enough for her to make it to the sanctuary of her own flat afterwards. At least he had not demanded to see her in her own home.

She joined him as calmly as possible, trying to ignore the hint of colour in her cheeks, pulling on her leather gloves, the briefcase under her arm.

'Delectable,' he said in that amused, caressing voice.

She did not answer verbally, her raised eyebrow querying the remark.

'The cool executive lady,' he explained, escorting her outside and putting her into the Mercedes. 'It's all right, George,' he added to the chauffeur. 'I'll drive myself.'

As the man tipped his hat and moved off into the building, Raoul went on reflectively, 'It makes me want to rip your clothes off and see if you stay as cool. A challenge you might say. I wonder if the clients feel the same. Perhaps that's the secret of your success. What do you think?'

Philippa was speechless, her thoughts in turmoil. His words conjured up memories of when she had not stayed cool at all and he must know it. He was doing it deliberately, trying to throw her off balance, to embarrass her. And he was succeeding. She was going to have to be very careful this evening.

Overcoming the constriction in her throat, she said coldly. 'I think you enjoy being mischievous.'

He made no answer to that, beyond a quick impatient sigh and turned the powerful car into the stream of traffic. Philippa stared resolutely out of the window the while, fixing her eyes on the brightly lit shops with their festive windows already dressed for Christmas. Her eyes blurred but she resolutely refused to dab at them and widened her gaze to dispel the blurring of vision caused by impending tears. Whatever else she did this evening, she was not going to cry over him, she promised herself.

So deep was she in her unhappy reflections that she did not notice for several minutes that they were moving out on the western arterial road, away from the centre of London. And Raoul, she was fairly certain, always stayed at the Ritz when he was in London.

'You have missed the turning,' she said, swinging round in her seat to see what traffic was behind them. 'What a nuisance. I suppose it is difficult negotiating all the one way systems in the dark. Especially as you're not a native,' she added sympathetically.

He gave a little choke of laughter. 'You're very charitable. But I haven't missed my way.'

She stared at him in the intermittent darkness of the car.

'You didn't ask which hotel I intended to take you to,' he reminded her gently.

'Where are we going?' demanded Philippa in a strangled voice.

Raoul was bland. 'I'm taking a few days off. I thought a little break in the countryside would be nice.'

She caught her breath. 'Where?'

'Caple Penny,' he told her cheerfully. 'It's a tiny hamlet in the Cotswolds. With a superb village pub. I promise you, the food will be out of this world. And the peace,' he added kindly, 'will be good for you.'

'Stop the car,' said Philippa. 'I'm not going along with this.'

'But if you had only asked which hotel I was staying in I would have told you,' Raoul said. 'I can't stop now. And you certainly can't hitch-hike back to the West End. You might get some very unacceptable propositions.'

'I thought you meant London as you very well know,' she snapped.

'Then you should have said so.' The token regret in his voice was an insult in itself. Underneath, she realised, he was gleeful. He added in a different voice, 'I think that's another round to me, don't you?'

She turned her shoulder on him, refusing to answer. And though he chatted away in an unconcerned manner for the rest of the journey she did not answer him by so much as a sniff.

But she was not so innocent as to be unprepared for what was to happen when they arrived at The White Hart. It was a cheerful place, full of blazing log fires and a fair number of people, presumably local, gathered in the low beamed bar. The manager bustled up to them, welcoming but busy and clearly not wanting to stay and discuss their accommodation.

'De Martin? Ah yes, Monsieur and Madame. Your secretary booked earlier. If you would like to go up and make yourselves comfortable? As you see we are busy tonight. You can sign the register tomorrow.' He summoned a bellboy who collected two suitcases from the boot of the Mercedes, Philippa saw with resignation. Raoul left nothing to chance. She wondered whether he had filled the second one with clothes she had left behind in the château and found herself desperately hoping that he had not.

'You will be dining in your suite, yes? A good thing, if you're tired. We're beginning to get the Christmas celebration trade,' the manager said chattily. 'You will find a menu in your room. Just phone down your order when you are ready.'

The room was on the second floor. Wooden panelled and chintz hung, it looked more like something from a historical film set than a hotel room, Philippa thought. To enter it you had to go down three polished wooden steps. She almost fell down them, her eyes riveted on the mahogany four poster that dominated the floor.

'Careful,' murmured Raoul, catching her elbow with iron fingers and restoring her solicitously to an upright position. 'They're deceptive those steps. You have to work to keep your balance.'

She tore her arm away, giving him a look of burning reproach. The bellboy, gratefully receiving his tip, might not realise it but she knew exactly how double edged that last remark was. She backed away from him.

'All right,' she said, her voice high and frightened. 'I concede the next round. Now what happens?'

Raoul considered her thoughtfully. 'That depends.'

Her laugh had more than a touch of hysteria in it.

'On what?'

'On whether you concede the whole game,' he told her pleasantly.

She fought for composure. 'If I knew what game we were playing—or what the stakes are—I might be able to tell you,' she said lightly.

A flash of admiration lit his eyes, she thought, but she might have been mistaken, for in an instant it was gone and he was his usual self, negligent, mocking and acute as a cat.

'The game,' he said wryly, 'is, for want of a better word, marriage. And you are the stakes.'

She whitened, retreating from him as if from a torturer. Seeing it, he frowned swiftly but he did not follow her across the room. Instead he flung himself on to a curlicued chair and tossed his jacket aside.

'You see, I make no bones about it. I want you. I have always wanted you. I didn't win you fairly in the first place. And,' his voice grew grim, 'I'll play very dirty indeed to get you back.'

He was appallingly attractive, lounging there, the piercing eyes half hidden by heavy eyelids, the firm, sensual mouth set in a hard line. Philippa knew a great surge of longing to touch her lips in a thousand butterfly kisses over the cold and handsome face. Her whole body ached for him with an intensity which was frightening. She did not know how much longer she could maintain the pretence of composure.

'What do you want of me?' she asked in despair.

Raoul's eyes glinted in his swift, upward look. 'Everything. Body and soul. Heart and mind. I am not,' he explained, 'a moderate man. I want all of you.'

She was shaken. She knew he was attracted to her; there had never been any mistaking the blinding magnetism between them. But she had never before looked at him and seen naked craving in his face.

'Why?' she almost cried, wringing her hands.

He shrugged at that, the light dancing over his golden head so that he reminded her again of one of the golden statues of the ancient world. He was so beautiful, so classically handsome. He could have anyone he set his mind to: why did he need to torment her?

She sat down on the edge of the high bed, trying to gather her forces, muster her arguments. She had nothing now to rely on for her escape but her native wit and, pitted against his uncompromising tactics, she did not rate highly her chances of getting away from him. But before she succumbed utterly to her agonising love for him she had to make one last attempt to get free, to set him free, too, from the consequences of her unwanted devotion.

'Raoul, when I married you I did not want to marry at all. Not you. Not anyone,' she said with difficulty.

There was a flash of something in his eyes which she could not interpret.

'Are you trying to tell me it's nothing personal?' Raoul asked, amused.

She smiled briefly at the sally but went doggedly on, 'I'd always led rather a self-contained life.'

She paused, looking down at her hands, unnaturally still in her lap. Raoul, she knew, was watching her, his gaze never shifting from her bent head.

'Don't misunderstand me. I wasn't lonely. I lived like that because I wanted to. My experience of men had not been very happy. I never thought I would marry.'

Raoul swore softly and virulently. Startled, Philippa raised her head. The gaze was still fixed intensely on her but the eyes were black with fury.

She said in panic, 'I'm sorry. I should have told you.' The words were tumbling over each other in her haste to excuse herself. 'Should have said there'd been somebody else ... that I wasn't available for a real marriage, that I wouldn't ever have been ...'

Raoul said bitingly, 'Do I take it that you have at last decided to tell all about your cousin Rupert?'

This was so unexpected that Philippa could only gaze at him, open mouthed.

'Don't look at me like that,' he said, shaken with furious impatience. 'Did you think I didn't know? I've known from the first. Your good aunt made damn sure I knew.'

She shook her head in bewilderment. 'Aunt Margaret?'

'You have others? How lucky I am not to have met them!' His tone was savage. 'Yes. As soon as I made it plain that I—was attracted to you, she told me that you were head-over-heels in love with your cousin and had been since you were a child.'

'B-but why should she do such a thing?' she said numbly.

Raoul shrugged. 'To put me in my place, I imagine. She certainly enjoyed it.'

Philippa bit her lip. That made sense. Aunt Margaret had been furiously resentful of the intruding Frenchman's influence over Uncle David. She had thought he was usurping Rupert's rightful place. And the fact that Rupert's father acquiesced willingly in Rupert's loss of influence had left Aunt Margaret feeling that Raoul was the enemy and she was her darling's only champion. Philippa could well imagine her aunt, in that mood, spitefully telling Raoul that he would never be able to compete with Rupert in his cousin's affections.

But, even to score a point, Aunt Margaret had never been a liar. And she knew perfectly well that the only man in Philippa's life had been Bob Sebastian. Even as adolescents, Philippa and Rupert had been good friends; there was never any possibility of attraction between them.

She said slowly, 'You must have misunderstood her.'

His laugh was harsh. 'Oh, there was no misunderstanding. She made sure of that. She told me at length how you were devoted to him, how the poor boy was embarrassed by it but always let you down lightly, how you'd only gone to work in the family firm to be near him . . .'

Philippa's gaze was wrenched to his. *'What?'*

'How you worked for Vivian just to be close to Rupert Vivian,' he repeated with more than a hint of a snap. 'Oh, it was all done very delicately, of course, but the implication was obvious: if there was no Rupert Vivian there, then you would take yourself off to wherever he chose to exercise his dubious talents.'

'I see,' she said, her brow clearing.

No, Aunt Margaret would not tell a lie for simple spite. But to protect Rupert's future, his job, which she had every reason to believe was threatened, yes Aunt Margaret would use whatever tool she could lay her hands on to do that.

'And as I had realised that you were pretty well indispensable to the company—quite apart from what I felt for you myself—I realised that Rupert had to stay. Particularly after I heard you were talking to Caverdons about a new job.'

Philippa stared at him. 'You're well informed.'

His smile was wry. 'Darling, in your case it's taken all the self-control I possess not have a twenty-four-hour tail on you. It seemed the whole world wanted to tell me about you and Rupert: how he'd tried to marry you off to one of his friends but you turned him down. How you protected him in the firm. Even when you went out for a drink together, for God's sake. Your aunt's thesis was that you were drowning your sorrows in work and would never look at a man again.' He paused. 'From my own observation, it did not seem improbable.'

Philippa said, 'I have never heard such melodramatic nonsense in my life.'

'Then why wouldn't you give us a chance? Why wouldn't you let me get close to you? Even after we were married, why did you keep fighting me off?' demanded Raoul in despair.

Philippa swallowed. It would be so easy to bring down all her defences; to tell him the truth flatly, now, without any more pretence. Because I am in love with you, have been in love with you for weeks. Because I didn't dare to put that weapon in your hands. But she could not. Raoul sighed.

'Philippa?'

He stood up and went to the window, his hands in his

pockets. Without turning his head he said unemotionally, 'We are both adult, intelligent people. It is in both our interests to make this marriage work. I am trying to find out what is preventing it. I,' a ghost of self-mockery, 'am willing enough. It is you who obstruct it. I have a right to know why.'

She could not deny it. She clasped the bedpost tighter, biting her lip.

'Do you think that Rupert would have wanted you if you had not been my wife?' he went on, in the still, deadly voice. 'Do you think that, if I give you the divorce you want, he will marry you? I can tell you he won't.'

'No,' she said in a strangled voice, horrified at his words.

'He sees me as a successful rival, of course. He has a competitive streak, so he thought it would be amusing to win you back. But he will lose interest when he thinks I am no longer interested. You would do better,' the soft voice bit, 'to settle for stable marriage and a regular income. Rupert is not going to provide either.'

Suddenly Philippa was very angry. She let go the bedpost and sat up straight.

'Not for me, certainly,' she said coolly. 'I wouldn't want him to.'

'You prefer the heady romance of a clandestine affair?' he mocked.

'I prefer,' said Philippa between her teeth, 'a stable single life and a regular income I earn for myself. I don't need to take your bullying and your insults and your damned high-handed ways. I won't put up with them. I don't know whether you want me to come back and have an affair with Rupert in France, or whether you've reverted to your original plan and prefer me to take Alex Januar as my lover, but I can tell you now, I won't tolerate either.'

'What?' He whipped round, his face quite blank.

'Oh, did you think I wouldn't find out?' Philippa taunted him. She had the upper hand for once and she was not going to be intimidated any more. 'I suppose usually you just make up your mind what people are going to do and the poor fools patter off and do it. Well, not me.'

He said in a whisper, 'What are you talking about?'

She laughed. 'The grand strategic plan that had me paired off with Alex while you did whatever seemed good to you with Sally Sebastian.'

He took a hasty step forward. 'I have never in my life hit a woman,' Raoul told her softly, 'and it may have been a mistake.'

She tossed her head, meeting his furious eyes with an expression as angry as his own.

'Are you seriously suggesting that I set up a—a—a liaison between you and Alex?'

'I asked you,' she pointed out, quivering with rage. 'And you agreed. And when I was—quite justifiably— upset you thought I was making a fuss about nothing and said it was a *compliment*.' She spat the last word at him with all the venom of weeks of suppressed indignation.

Raoul was stunned. He stared at her, the fury visibly draining from his body. Then, unforgivably, the golden eyes began to gleam and he started to shake with laughter.

'How dare you?' she hissed, insulted beyond measure.

He flung up a hand. 'No don't hit me, my darling. Not again. You nearly laid me out that night on the terrace.' He stopped laughing and sobered, though there was a distinct thread of amusement in his voice still. 'I don't know where you got your extraordinary idea from, my angel, but we have been at cross purposes it would seem. When we last spoke about Alex I thought you were making a fuss about having your portrait painted. The fuss was not unexpected, because you have always been a difficult customer,' he explained, his eyes glinting, 'though I confess I thought the intensity of your objections a bit excessive in the circumstances.' He almost laughed again but restrained himself, 'Now, of course, I see why. Alex Januar is one of the more distinguished portraitists of our time,' he explained with odious patience. 'I was rather pleased with myself for having persuaded him to paint you. Not, as it turns out, one of my more inspired projects.'

He reached out and took her competently into his arms. Philippa went unresisting.

'Portrait?' she said blankly.

'Yup,' he was touching his mouth very softly to the tender skin of her neck just below her ear. She made no protest, her mind still occupied with the enormity of her discovery.

'But you said—when I asked you—you said you had brought Alex Januar to the château for me. You said he was supposed to persuade me.'

'Mmm,' Raoul settled her comfortably against his body and continued his leisurely exploration of her throat. 'To sit for him, darling one,' he murmured against her skin, his body shaking with laughter. 'Only to sit for him.'

'But why didn't you *say* so?'

'I thought I had. It never occurred to me you would not recognise Alex. Sally and Rupert certainly did.'

Philippa jumped. 'Did they?'

Had Rupert deliberately misled her? He was capable of making mischief, she knew. And yet he had seemed so genuinely sorry for her. Almost guilty, she had thought, as if in some way he held himself responsible for her plight. She shook her head in bewilderment.

'I think you owe me an apology,' Raoul said, amused but determined.

She found her jacket had been slipped competently from her and her blouse was going the same way. His cool hands on her flesh were infinitely soothing, beguiling. She knew it was a trap. She fought away.

'I'll apologise in writing,' she said breathlessly, easing herself round the fourposter bed.

The golden eyes gleamed. 'I won't insist on that,' Raoul told her smoothly, following her.

'Raoul, I don't want to go to bed with you,' she said desperately.

If she thought he would halt at that, she was mistaken. His smile grew and one wicked eyebrow rose.

'My dear girl, you know quite well that all the way down here in the car neither you nor I was thinking about anything else.'

Philippa made an infuriated little noise and, if she had not recalled herself in time, would have stamped her foot. That it was true, made the cheerful remark no easier to bear. She retreated further until her back was against the bedside table thoughtfully provided by the management.

Without undue haste but with no sign of being gainsaid either, Raoul trod softly after her. In his face she read a good humoured implacability which she knew she could not deflect. It would happen then; she was defeated. She could not go into his arms again and deny her starved love.

As he reached for her purposefully, she gave a small sob, quickly suppressed.

'Ah, don't cry,' he said, holding her hard against him. 'You never cry, my lovely one. Don't cry now.'

'I c . . . can't help it,' she sniffed. 'I'm sorry. I feel a fool.'

He pushed her head down into his shoulder and stroked her hair with fingers that shook. Philippa only registered it slowly and when she did she lifted her head and stared at him incredulously. The good humour, she found, was only skin deep. Beneath it he looked as if he was under intolerable strain and had been for weeks. And he looked defeated. His hands fell away.

'Is Sally right then?' he said, almost to himself. 'Have I made you afraid of me?'

At the mention of Sally Sebastian's name, Philippa froze. So they had discussed her. Pityingly, no doubt. She went to the dressing table, picking up a comb and dragging it through her tumbled hair with a hand that was not quite steady. He watched her gravely.

At last he said, 'I wondered what you were afraid of, that last weekend. I thought you were nervous about being found out in your affair with Rupert. But afterwards, I thought about it. How you'd said you hated me.' He paused. 'It was me you were afraid of, wasn't it?'

Philippa found she could not speak. The comb fell with a clatter on to the glass-topped dressing table. She stared at him in the mirror. His mouth had taken on that bitter twist.

'I think,' he said reflectively, 'that that was when I gave up hope really. Though of course, I haven't admitted it.'

He rose and she tensed but he was only looking for his cigarette case in his jacket pocket. He extracted a cigarette and lit it with care, before seating himself in a solid chair, arranging an ashtray with compulsive symmetry on its arm. He leaned back against the cushions, watching her reflected face.

'I knew there was a lot to overcome, of course,' he went on, almost conversationally. 'I knew you were frightened of having your privacy invaded. I knew you were resentful of the way I had bulldozed you into marriage. I found out,' his expression was wry, 'rather later than I would have liked, that you were not the experienced woman everyone told me you were.' He drew on his cigarette, his eyes watchful behind the thin column of smoke. 'But it also seemed to me that, even in spite of yourself, you were half-way there. When we made love,' he explained, in case she misunderstood.

Philippa flushed. She had given herself away all right. Perhaps from the start. Certainly on that last, shattering occasion, he could not have mistaken her desperate longing for his love. She shuddered and could not look at him.

He drew on the cigarette again.

'You know, when you first told me that it was no better than rape, I didn't believe you.'

He ground the cigarette, less than half smoked, into the bronze ashtray with savage movements, at variance with his controlled pose and light, indifferent voice. Philippa turned to face him, bracing herself against the furniture behind her.

'But it's true, isn't it? You can't bear me to touch you. Even now, you're shaking,' he said sadly. 'I'm— sorry. God knows I never meant . . .'

The lines round his mouth were deep slashes. Philippa found that she could not bear the look of pain in his eyes.

She flushed but met his gaze steadily. 'I want you to touch me all the time,' she told him with the calm of despair. 'And you must know that.'

The golden eyes flared and then narrowed.

'You loathe me. You said so, last time. I haven't forgotten that.'

Nothing mattered but that he should not look so bitter.

'I lied,' she said harshly.

There was a long silence. Philippa's wrists ached with tension where they were crushed against the edge of the dressing table.

Still he did not speak. She realised that more was required of her, that he still believed he had frightened and hurt her. That he was torn by a self disgust which only a full confession on her part could relieve him of.

She swallowed hard and said with real courage, 'Raoul, I am very sorry but I am in love with you. It's not your fault and you don't have to do anything about it. But that is why I can't bear you to touch me. Because it doesn't mean anything. For you that is. And for me it means . . .' her voice was suspended but brought it back under control and managed to say evenly, 'too much.'

She could not look him in the face. He sat as if turned to stone. Then the ashtray went spinning from its perch as he rose so violently that the chair span away from him across the polished floorboards. Philippa shut her eyes.

'What did you say?' he said in a whisper.

But she could not repeat it. She shook her head, trying to still her trembling lips.

'You fool.' He was furious. There was no doubt of it. 'You blind, stupid, devious, complicated *fool.*'

She was seized off her feet and flung unceremoniously into the middle of the counterpane. And he was beside her, kissing her savagely, remorselessly.

'Dear God, don't you understand?' He took her face between his hands and forced her to look at him. 'Don't you understand anything? I have been sick with love for you more or less since we first met. I've lied and cheated and bullied and blackmailed and locked you up, for no other reason. How dare you say it doesn't mean anything for me to make love to you? How dare you?'

'B-but . . .' Philippa found that she believed him but could not prevent the question that had embittered so many months for her, 'but you were still taking out

Sally Sabastian. She was your mistress. She told Rupert so.'

Raoul sighed. 'My dear, dim darling, have you not noticed that your cousin Rupert is mad about Sally? If she told him anything of the sort—which doesn't sound her style at all, mind you—it would be to shake him up. He's too much of playboy for a professional working woman like Sally. Though I suspect she is more than fond of him, underneath.'

Philippa considered this. It was feasible. It was even likely. Had she not thought herself that Rupert had seemed jealous of Raoul? And he had even admitted to her that he was in love with Sally.

'I've been very stupid,' she said remorsefully.

'Yes,' Raoul agreed without chivalry. 'Intelligent women are always the most stupid. I suppose I shall get used to it.'

He began to kiss her lingeringly.

She wriggled with pleasure.

'Will you ever forgive me?'

His lips against her skin he said, 'After a hundred years or so.'

'Oh dear,' she teased. 'What can I say to make amends?'

Raoul raised his head and looked at her with a great display of patience. The golden eyes were so warm and loving that Philippa felt her heart would break with happiness.

'You're not supposed to say anything,' he complained. 'This is not the time for polite conversation.'

She laid her fingers against his mouth.

'Just let me say this, my love. When we met—when we married—you did frighten me, as you said. Because of what you could make me feel without me wanting it. I felt trapped.'

'And now?' Raoul asked soberly.

Philippa began to smile. 'Now I think we're both trapped and I don't mind so much. Or at all.' She reached up to kiss him. 'And I won't say another word,' she promised mischievously.

Which, in the circumstances, was sensible.

Coming Next Month in Harlequin Presents!

839 BITTER ENCORE—Helen Bianchin
Nothing can erase the memory of their shared passion. But can an estranged couple reunite when his star status still leaves no room for her in his life—except in his bed?

840 FANTASY—Emma Darcy
On a secluded beach near Sydney, a model, disillusioned by her fiancé, finds love in the arms of a stranger. Or is it all a dream—this man, this fantasy?

841 RENT-A-BRIDE LTD—Emma Goldrick
Fearful of being forced to marry her aunt's stepson, an heiress confides in a fellow passenger on her flight from Denver—never thinking he'd pass himself off as her new husband!

842 WHO'S BEEN SLEEPING IN MY BED?—Charlotte Lamb
The good-looking playwright trying to win her affection at the family villa in France asks too many questions about her father's affairs. She's sure he's using her.

843 STOLEN SUMMER—Anne Mather
She's five years older, a friend of the family's. And he's engaged! How can she take seriously a young man's amorous advances? Then again, how can she not?

844 LIGHTNING STORM—Anne McAllister
A young widow returns to California and re-encounters the man who rejected her years before—a man after a good time with no commitments. Does lightning really strike twice?

845 IMPASSE—Margaret Pargeter
Unable to live as his mistress, a woman left the man she loves. Now he desires her more than ever—enough, at least, to ruin her engagement to another man!

846 FRANGIPANI—Anne Weale
Her sister's offer to find her a millionaire before they dock in Fiji is distressing. She isn't interested. But the captain of the ship finds that hard to believe....

H·A·R·L·E·Q·U·I·N

FIRST·CLASS
Sweepstakes

OFFICIAL RULES

1. NO PURCHASE NECESSARY. To enter, complete the official entry/order form. Be sure to indicate whether or not you wish to take advantage of our subscription offer.

2. Entry blanks have been preselected for the prizes offered. Your response will be checked to see if you are a winner. In the event that these preselected responses are not claimed, a random drawing will be held from all entries received to award not less than $150,000 in prizes. This is in addition to any free, surprise or mystery gifts which might be offered. Versions of this sweepstakes with different prizes will appear in Preview Service Mailings by Harlequin Books and their affiliates. Winners selected will receive the prize offered in their sweepstakes brochure.

3. This promotion is being conducted under the supervision of Marden-Kane, an independent judging organization. By entering the sweepstakes, each entrant accepts and agrees to be bound by these rules and the decisions of the judges, which shall be final and binding. Odds of winning in the random drawing are dependent upon the total number of entries received. Taxes, if any, are the sole responsibility of the prize winners. Prizes are nontransferable. All entries must be received by August 31, 1986.

4. The following prizes will be awarded:

    (1) Grand Prize: Rolls-Royce™ *or* $100,000 Cash!
    (Rolls-Royce being offered by permission of
    Rolls-Royce Motors Inc.)

    (1) Second Prize: A trip for two to Paris for 7 days/6 nights. Trip includes air transportation on the Concorde, hotel accommodations...PLUS...$5,000 spending money!

    (1) Third Prize: A luxurious Mink Coat!

5. This offer is open to residents of the U.S. and Canada, 18 years or older, except employees of Harlequin Books, its affiliates, subsidiaries, Marden-Kane and all other agencies and persons connected with conducting this sweepstakes. All Federal, State and local laws apply. Void in the province of Quebec and wherever prohibited or restricted by law. Winners will be notified by mail and may be required to execute an affidavit of eligibility and release, which must be returned within 14 days after notification. Canadian winners will be required to answer a skill-testing question. Winners consent to the use of their name, photograph and/or likeness for advertising and publicity purposes in conjunction with this and similar promotions without additional compensation. One prize per family or household.

6. For a list of our most current prize winners, send a stamped, self-addressed envelope to: WINNERS LIST, c/o Marden-Kane, P.O. Box 10404, Long Island City, New York 11101

Here's how to get this special offer from Harlequin! As simple as 1...2...3!

NOVEMBER
TREASURY EDITION
COUPON

1. Each month, save one Treasury Edition coupon from your favorite Romance or Presents novel.
2. In four months you'll have saved four Treasury Edition coupons (<u>only one coupon per month allowed</u>).
3. Then all you have to do is fill out and return the order form provided, along with the four Treasury Edition coupons required and $1.00 for postage and handling.

Mail to: Harlequin Reader Service

In the U.S.A.
2504 West Southern Ave.
Tempe, AZ 85282

In Canada
P.O. Box 2800, Postal Station A
5170 Yonge Street
Willowdale, Ont. M2N 6J3

RT1-D-2

Please send me my FREE copy of the Janet Dailey Treasury Edition. I have enclosed the four Treasury Edition coupons required and $1.00 for postage and handling along with this order form.

(Please Print)

NAME_____

ADDRESS_____

CITY_____

STATE/PROV._____ ZIP/POSTAL CODE_____

SIGNATURE_____

This offer is limited to one order per household.

SUPPLIES LIMITED

This special Janet Dailey offer expires January 1986.

Take 4 books & a surprise gift FREE

SPECIAL LIMITED-TIME OFFER

Mail to   **Harlequin Reader Service®**

In the U.S.
2504 West Southern Ave.
Tempe, AZ 85282

In Canada
P.O. Box 2800, Station "A"
5170 Yonge Street
Willowdale, Ontario M2N 6J3

YES! Please send me 4 free Harlequin Presents® novels and my free surprise gift. Then send me 8 brand-new novels every month as they come off the presses. Bill me at the low price of $1.75 each ($1.95 in Canada)—a 11% saving off the retail price. There are no shipping, handling or other hidden costs. There is no minimum number of books I must purchase. I can always return a shipment and cancel at any time. Even if I never buy another book from Harlequin, the 4 free novels and the surprise gift are mine to keep forever.

Name _____ (PLEASE PRINT) _____

Address _____ Apt. No. _____

City _____ State/Prov. _____ Zip/Postal Code _____

This offer is limited to one order per household and not valid to present subscribers. Price is subject to change.

DOP–SUB–1